That One Day in August

REBECCA GRAVES

RAVEN RANCH PRESS
Vashon, Washington

Comments and inquiries regarding this book
may be sent to the author at *corner48@comcast.net*

ISBN-13: 978-0991659210
Library of Congress Control Number: 2019909444

Published by:
Raven Ranch Press
Vashon Island, Washington

Book Layout & Design:
Natalie Kosovac
Natfly Productions

Editing & Proofreading:
Nancy Morgan
Eagle Eye Proofreading & Editing

Cover Art:
Tie-dye garment
by Rod Smith

Back Cover Art:
Islewilde maypole photo
flickr.com/photos/islewilde/

RAVEN RANCH PRESS
Vashon, Washington

Dedicated to all the lovely, quirky, and colorful people of Vashon Island.

Foreword

On the occasion of the confluence of events on that one day in August 1996, a germ of an idea occurred to me. I said to myself, "Somebody should write a book about that." And I sat down and wrote one or two pages about Leni. Then it sat in a pile of papers for 20 years. Fast forward to a few years ago when I was invited to join a small cadre of friends in a writing group. I unearthed that germ (yes, I still had the very pile) and as I looked at it, I thought, "Well, I guess that would be something I could Wooorrrkkk on," like it would be hard. In fact it turned out not to be hard at all. I have heard authors say that their characters take over and direct the writing but I never believed it. Yet that is exactly what happened. These wonderful, wacky people were apparently just hanging out in my head, waiting for me to tell their story. After I related this decades-long background to a writer friend, she commented that it evidently had been baking, or proofing, as in yeast rising. It seems she was right.

This is a work of fiction. Any similarity to actual people or events is purely coincidental, except when it's not. All the main characters are made up, although perhaps inspired by a real person. Some of the minor ones are familiar and beloved island characters whose names I have changed a tiny bit. All is meant in the spirit of love.

I have no idea if there ever was a toymaker's product that played a cassette tape for an alarm, I made that up. But it seemed believable, like there might have been, or could have been.

Leni

"Allons enfants de la patrie, le jour de gloire est arrivé. . . ."

Strains of "La Marseillaise" blasting from Leni's alarm woke her earlier than usual. Never happy about rising, she growled and groped her way to the bathroom and then to the kitchen.

"I could use a day of glory," she thought groggily to herself, listening all the way to the end of the song, as was her habit. She never tired of hearing the stirring French Revolution anthem calling on the citizenry to rise up. She opened the freezer, grabbed the partially frozen Coke, and stumbled out onto the deck, lighting up a Pall Mall on the way. After a few deep drags on both the cigarette and the soda, she began to come awake a little. This had been her morning routine since college and she saw no reason to change it. There was too much change in the world today without her contributing to it, though she had made one small concession—the Coke was now a Diet Coke.

She needed to get up to town and open the shop early today so that she could set up the sidewalk sale for the Dog Days event the Chamber of Commerce had practically forced her to participate in. Normally her business did not have a sidewalk sale, as it did not really carry the kind of inventory that attracts crowds. Leni owned a ceramics store, the kind where people come in, choose from the various greenware molds, buy brushes and glazes, and sit there and paint it, then come back to pick it up after Leni fires it for them. It was not at all what she had envisioned herself doing, but oh the surprises that life holds for us. Having Maryka was one of the biggest.

Leni considered herself a feminist in college, before that term was really even in use. Thought she knew about birth control, but apparently there were nuances. When push came to shove, she found herself unable to choose abortion, and so Maryka was born. Her real name is Mary Kay, named after her grandmother, Leni's mom, who passed the ceramics shop on to Leni so she could support herself and a child. It's a business where a baby could hang out. In fact, it attracted the grandmotherly types who like sitting and painting ceramic angels and leprechauns and a million other tchotchkes while watching over the adorable baby. So Leni never quite finished her degree, though her studies never waned. Her customers got to know a lot about the French Revolution, Leni's "major," while Maryka learned to toddle about keeping her hands off the oh-so-fragile greenware molds.

Remembering that she had forgotten to pee upon waking (the stop at the bathroom had just been for a brief glance around the room), Leni finished her cigarette and went back inside, noting as she opened the screen door that one corner was flapping open, and therefore not very useful at all in keeping the flies and mosquitoes out. She sighed. One more thing to think about fixing. Washing her hands and face, she inspected herself in the bathroom mirror. Same straw-colored frizzled hair in a "care-free" style she had in college, same intense blue eyes that could drill holes in a person. She had not aged all that well. Unbidden, an image of her internal organs looking as shriveled and old as her complexion appeared on her inner monitor. A flicker of something arced across a corner of her consciousness, reminding her that in a couple of years she would reach the cultural milestone of the BIG 5-0, and my, hadn't she better do something about that face? Quickly she shoved that thought back down whence it came.

She went back into the bedroom and sat down on the unmade tangle of sheets, turned to the "alarm clock"—a thing someone not in the immediate family had given Maryka on one of her birthdays, a combination simple radio function of alarm clock and a cassette tape player, so that it could be programmed to play whatever tape was in it at a certain time (it may have been Fisher-Price or Mattel, a product that was eventually abandoned because it never caught on)—and popped the lid open to rewind the tape, which she had to do every single morning. Her tape of the French Revolution music was old and the sound was pretty scratchy on the rudimentary equipment, but Leni remained devoted to the cause forever.

. . . The phone jangled on its purple ceramic cake platter, where it sat among a clutter of paper clips, post-it notes, one short dull pencil, and several nice little shells and rocks.

"Ma? Is there any way I could use your car this morning? The Hairnet isn't up to the task today." The Hairnet was a Hornet, a '70s era AMC model that was still drivable in the same sense that an octogenarian with severe arthritis in both hips was still ambulatory. Leni had bought it for her for $50 when Maryka got her driver's license six years ago, and with lots of help from a generous mechanic friend, it was still running, sort of.

Leni sighed. She could have foreseen this.

Walking back outside, she squinted down at the little house below the deck and about 50 feet to the west. The B frame, as they referred to it—an auxiliary house converted from a shop into a dwelling—was actually almost nicer than the main house, the A frame, where Leni lived, though both were, on the spectrum of homes, closer to the shack end than the mansion end. The A frame badly needed a deck rebuild, and Leni's attempts at landscaping had failed so many times she had given up. There was a nice latticework trellis archway devoid of any vegetation standing as a testament to the many clematises Leni had killed. Otherwise there were several varieties of hearty plants that thrived on neglect and the deer didn't care for—a rock rose the size of a Volkswagen Beetle, dead around the bottom edges and which partially blocked the view of the house, giving Maryka and Dïm a modicum of privacy, a thirsty hydrangea, and lots of California poppies—overgrown with grass that had turned brown for the duration.

"Where's Dïm?" Leni inquired in a tone that attempted to be neutral but somehow included a smidgeon of accusatory inflection.

"He already left with the van to take the tables and stuff up to the park. Remember? It's the We Are All One World Fair?" (Duh?)

"I know, I know it's the WAAOW Fair." Leni pronounced the acronym to rhyme with meow, which she thought a clever little play of language considering her next remark. "Do you also remember that it's Dog Days? I have to go to town in about a half hour. And do you also know that it's the goddamned Republican Picnic today? Do you realize what the traffic is going to be like? That's right across the road from your WAAOW Fair, Missy." This time she said it with a hint of wimpy cat inflection.

Leni had become one of those mothers she looked down upon before she had a child—the ones who use nicknames for their children, like Bubba and Sissy. But Mary Kay had seemed such a long moniker for a teeny baby that Leni found herself falling into the habit of calling her Missy. And then later, when teenaged Mary Kay rebelled against her name because it was the name of a makeup company (Ew), they had compromised and come up with Maryka, but Missy was the default name Leni fell back on when stressed.

"Well geez, Mom, you don't have to be that upset. You won't be out in the traffic, and maybe you'll get some more business because of it. And the Republican picnic has a shuttle bus from the field down the road where they've set up a parking lot, AND from the ferry by the way, so there won't really be that much traffic anyway."

Ah yes. The ever serene ones. Take the best view of things. Accept. Go with the flow. Dïm (pronounced Deem), or Dim, as she sometimes referred to him in the privacy of her mind, was Maryka's boyfriend hailing from some vaguely India-ish country but Leni could never remember which one. Why, she lamented, could he not be one of the hordes of bright, motivated, ambitious Asian students flocking to this country to take over our tech industries and make a fortune? But no, he was going down the Gandhi/Buddha path. He taught meditation classes at the gym. Plus he created sand mandalas. Thus, it was mostly up to Maryka to be the breadwinner. She taught preschool part-time. The rent was free, so between the pair they could almost keep themselves operational, barring major unexpected expenses.

Leni looked down at the B frame again. Maryka had stepped outside and was looking up at her with her palms up as if to say "What is the problem?"

"Oh. Well. I guess I can ask Hank if I can borrow one of his cars to take to town. But honestly . . ."

"Mom! Do NOT start up with the whenareyougoingtogetarealcar stuff again, please! Just not right now—I really have to go. Dïm forgot his bin of red sand and he needs it right away to start his mandala. You know Hank will fall all over himself to help you with any little thing you need."

This was true. Hank, the generous mechanic friend that had kept the Hairnet running all this time, had been in love with Leni ever since she had come back to the island and had the baby. But Leni had wanted fiercely to prove to the world that she could make it on her own with a kid, so she had held him at bay for almost 25 years. How had so much time passed? She allowed him to take her to dinner and spend two nights a week with her, but that was her limit. And he let her select from his collection of working vehicles anything she needed when Maryka borrowed Leni's Toyota, which was often enough.

Leni turned and peered off in the other direction, though nothing of Hank's rag-tag assortment of motors could be seen because of the trees between them. She sighed again.

"Well you might need to put some gas in it. I can't remember how close it is to empty."

"That's fine. I got paid yesterday."

"Are you going to be there all day?"

"Mom. It goes all day and then the potluck and then the music all evening."

"Right. Well just leave the key in the ignition when you get back then. I guess Hank and I will get some dinner someplace."

"I hear the Republican picnic is going to have some dynamite barbecue," Maryka teased.

"Very funny, Miss Bunny," shot back Leni with one of their old repartee bits.

"Not so much, Rabbit Hutch," came the automatic reply.

"Okay, time to get this jalopy in gear. I have places to go, people to see." And with that she hung up the phone, waved gaily to her daughter, and went inside to pee again.

* *

Hank

A hundred yards from Leni's A frame, but separated by a wooded stretch, was Hank's domain, where he lived and worked. The "yard" was littered with cars and trucks mostly, and perhaps the occasional repurposed school bus or flatbed made into an RV. Surrounded by scattered motors, transmissions, oil drums, and other accoutrements of a mechanic's world, Hank serenely plied his trade under a 12x20' canopy, his only concession to the continuously drippy skies of the Pacific Northwest. When he reached a good stopping place, or sometimes at 5:00 on the dot, depending on the day, he would reach for the rag in the pocket of his grease monkey suit, wipe his hands, and hang it up.

Then he would stretch, light up a joint, and toke on it while strolling toward a clump of scrub alders a little ways off. Half screened by those alders was a vintage camper trailer of the type that women swoon over and call "darling." Perfectly restored, it was 24' of curves and wood paneling, with shutters at the windows and a modest cedar deck overhung by a forest green awning. Two Adirondack chairs and a small round table comprised the deck furnishings, accessorized by an abundance of pots bursting with red and pink geraniums in full flower. In a sunny patch near the deck, two half whiskey barrels held robust cannabis plants.

The inside was all wood paneling and cabinetry, with cozy rugs and pillows in warm colors and soft lighting, curtains at the windows and some hanging spider plants, and it was immaculately neat and clean. There was the tiniest wood stove, no bigger than a hotplate, which kept the whole place toasty in cold weather. That was one thing that Hank wished was different—he would have liked a bigger stove, just because he loved dealing with the wood.

The smell of cedar kindling! So far from what he grew up with on the west Texas plain—Hank had found his true climate home when he came to the Northwest. He loved February because it was for him firewood season; Hank was fairly strict about cutting the wood before the sap started running. He admired the wood—the exquisite designs and colors of it. The fir rounds all yellow-orange on the ends with a rust red ring as the outer perimeter before the bark layer, then iced with a shaggy crop of emerald green moss. Or the madrone, with its glistening golden skin underneath the curling, peeling red bark; he remembered the first time he had seen that—unforgettable.

And the lichen! *Hypogymnia physodes*—the pale green paperlike lip-shaped lobes; *Platismatia stenophylla*—curvy clawed fingers reaching up and out, brown under green. Hank had been captivated by the myriad of mosses, and taken the trouble to study and learn some of their names. They were so beautiful he hated to whack them off the bark before splitting. He apologized to them in his mind. After all, he was killing colonies of living creatures. And then the split pieces of wood—the color and composition of some were breathtaking. Each piece completely unique. One yellow stripe outlined in brown in an otherwise pure white background. Some were twisted with a streak of pure rot down the middle. Hank reckoned that's where we got the terminology to describe some people. Some were on the way to that rot at the middle but turning an attractive shade of pinkish rust before arriving there, with perhaps a nice ripple effect for texture. Others had layers like geologic strata—ribbons of different colors, each pushing the next one up into hills and mountains. And once in a blue moon, that rarest of gifts—a round with grain so straight that at the first bite of the blade it springs apart with a single sharp pop, as clean as the snap of a gum bubble.

For his own enjoyment primarily then, Hank was happy to keep Leni's A frame supplied with wood for her airtight stove. He had an old tractor with a hydraulic splitter attachment, which he was always able to get working in time for firewood season. It was even something they did together—Leni would sit on a stool and run the lever that propelled the wood toward the blade and Hank would hoist up the rounds, examine each piece for the best way to position it, and maneuver it into place, then catch the four pieces before they fell. They both enjoyed it. Leni liked the leisure to sit and daydream (while still being vigilant about when to pull the lever back and push it forward), and gaze around wearing her rose-tinted sunglasses. The cerulean sky with a translucent quarter moon, the yellow-green new willow leaves in front of the dark green firs reaching up into the blue. One time they saw nine bald eagles soaring and gliding overhead. It was restorative. After several day sessions like this (stretched over weeks if the weather was bad), they had three cords of wood stacked in neat rows underneath the second-story deck. Hank loved watching the rows grow taller—he often went out of his way just to admire the progress of his firewood. And for the final step in the process of getting firewood to Leni's stove, he had rigged up an ingenious system of pulleys that could haul one of those corrugated steel watering troughs with handles on each end, full of wood, to the upper deck, something Leni could manage by herself. It was excellent.

On this Saturday morning, he was just finishing tidying up from breakfast when Leni knocked on the door, then opened it without waiting for him to answer.

"I need a car today," she said without preamble.

"Well and good morning to you too," he rumbled in his deep southern accent.

"Maryka needs to take mine—because of course Dïm forgot something he . . ."

"Spare me the details," he smiled, holding out a set of keys. "The dark red Subaru is road worthy as it happens." Hank disliked drama and did whatever he could to ignore it or disengage from it. He was content to exist in this little corner of the world and just get along with everybody. Leni thought that was unrealistic and escapist and frequently pointed that out to him. It was also a quality she was secretly attracted to.

"Well, I have to get up to town and put on the dog and pony show for the Chamber of Commerce. What are you doing today?" Hank often did not observe "regular" work week protocols with weekends and whatnot.

Hank shrugged. "I could be persuaded to be available for help if anyone needed help."

"Oh, and what would that take?" Leni flirted, all the while mentally scolding herself for acting in such a stereotypical manner. But Hank enjoyed it.

"Oh I don't know—maybe a promise of dinner tonight and a sleepover? It is Saturday after all."

"Hmmm, so it is. Well I guess I could commit to that." She tossed him an air kiss and turned on her heels. "Thanks for the ride."

"Hey wait—do you want help or not?"

"Well I guess, sure—I do have to tote all that stuff outside. Thanks." She paused. "You do know you're swell, right?"

Hank might have blushed a little, or possibly not.

Pete Kipp, but actually Nancy

Pete Kipp got up early Saturday morning, as was his habit. Years of athletic conditioning had made it difficult for him to lie about of a morning, a fact that his wife of 35 years sometimes decried. But then she was used to it. He was a college football player when they met and became sweethearts and then he had played pro football for many years before going into politics. And then their two sons became football players. Nancy Kipp was pretty much swallowed up by football like a speck of algae being surrounded by an amoeba. Her natural inclinations tended toward the slothful, and all these years she had had to generate enthusiasm for physical and sporty activities of all kinds just to stay in the mix. But she was getting to an age where she thought she might like to investigate more what people with her innate leanings did. More sedentary pursuits perhaps—genealogy, knitting, reading—really reading deep analyses of current events, and looking into the alternative side of things, the less mainstream things. Except now her husband was running for President.

The news of his running, when it came, was almost a visceral blow to Nancy, who had been hoping for a little slacking of the relentless scrutiny of their personal lives. She had already endured several campaigns of his to get elected to Congress, and it was no fun, believe you me, she would have said to anyone who asked. Sometimes she felt like such a fraud. How had she ended up in this position? Really, it was just that tiny indiscretion at that frat party that one time that had determined her whole life after that. Because then they felt obligated to marry, and they did love each other, truly they did, but what else might have been? She had gone to UC Berkeley and totally neglected to be a beatnik and smoke pot, for God's sake. And now it was too late.

Today held the promise of something at least not painful to endure—a picnic at a large estate on an island accessible only by ferry. Could even be fun, Nancy reasoned. At least there would probably be good food. Of course it was a fundraiser—their whole life was a fundraiser these days, and Nancy really hated that part. She had never been good at asking for money. She wasn't slated to speak today though, so perhaps she truly could just enjoy herself. If there was anyone there she could relate to. Really, Republicans these days. It would be a miracle if Pete won the nomination, being, as he was, a "bleeding heart conservative," meaning he had progressive ideas on labor and immigration and the economy. And if he did somehow secure the nomination, she didn't see how any Republican could win against the juggernaut that was Bill Clinton in 1996.

Nancy yawned and rolled over, then reluctantly threw off the covers and hauled herself up to a sitting position. Pete bounded into the bedroom. He still looked good, still had that square-jawed handsome All-American face, and of course kept himself in excellent shape. Nancy herself was inclined to hang out by the cocktail party tables with the Brie and the wine, and thus had chubbed up a wee bit since college days. She had to choose her clothes carefully to maximize her good points and minimize everything else.

"Baby! You're not up yet? Come on—we're catching a ferry in 45 minutes!"

"I know sweetie. I'll be ready in 15. After all the dress is fairly casual, right? I mean it is a picnic. Outside. Right?"

"Hmm?" He was checking his Palm Pilot. "Oh, right. Sure, just throw on some jeans and a blouse—you'll be fine." Pete had never been overly concerned with outward appearances, but then he always looked great, so he didn't have to be.

Sixteen minutes later Nancy was ready to go and their driver was waiting with the car at the front entrance of the hotel near the airport where they had spent the night. She won an approving glance from Nick, Pete's campaign manager, for her outfit—a red blazer over a white blouse with blue slacks, complete with striped scarf in the same colors. Inwardly she rolled her eyes. Just once she would like to wear something out of the ordinary.

* *

Dïm

Dïm's actual name was Vladïmir Petrovsky (Dïm being his nickname, the middle syllable of his name) and he was Pakistani, the offspring of a Russian army officer who defected from the Afghani struggle and went across the border to Peshawar, and an educated Pakistani woman—one of the very few—whose ambition was to work her way up through the ranks of Benazir Bhutto's government. Dïm had excelled in school and wanted to get the best education he could, which in his mind meant going to America. He had studied history, and astutely concluded that he had the best chance of surviving and living the Good Life if he did not live in the Middle East. His mother being in public service meant that she was able to pull some strings and get him a visa for the duration of his educational process. Dïm had no intention of going back, but he had not seen the need to discuss this with anyone so far.

Maryka had met him in college and he had stolen her heart as soon as she set eyes on him. Of course she couldn't help noticing right away that he was Omar Sharif-handsome, dark hair and eyes, and that honey-colored skin and the classic Russian bone structure of dancers. But beyond that there was a quality about him that was very intriguing. They met in a class entitled Digging into Process, an offering through the Psych department. Dïm had embarked on a combined bachelor's/master's in psychology program, and Maryka had enrolled in that course as one of her electives in an early childhood education degree.

Dïm was attracted to Maryka; her natural lithe grace and unique style of dress—draping tunics layered atop one another with varying hemlines slanting at interesting angles—reminded him vaguely of his homeland. He felt that she might be someone he could share things with, and indeed it turned out that she was. After only a few dates, they decided to move in together, which meant getting an apartment, since they both lived in the dorm. Because one of them had to have a driver's license and a checking account to sign the lease, Maryka was the one, which was the beginning of her dealing with the "real world" for both of them. But she didn't mind, for there was something endearing and childlike about him that she adored. He had a sense of wonderment and living in the present moment that just came naturally to him.

On the day they moved, Maryka had organized a small phalanx of friends and family to help. Of course Leni was there, and Hank had brought a large pickup truck. Maryka was in Dïm's room, helping him pack up his stuff, which he did not have much of, partially due to his not having brought much from Peshawar, but also because he was not that into amassing material goods. She picked up a plastic bottle of bubble blowing mixture and looked at Dïm quizzically.

"Is this yours?"

"Oh, yes," he said, looking slightly embarrassed.

"Do you still want it?"

"Most definitely," he said.

Maryka made a dubious "whatever" face and raised her eyebrows.

He grabbed both her hands. "Maryka, I must make a confession to you about that bubbles. I . . . I stole that. I am not a thief—you know that I am a good person, so please I beg you do not think poorly of me when you hear that. I stole that from the first grocery store I was in when I got to America. Because I had no money for such things, but I saw that and other things for having fun, and something in me just had to have it. Because in my country there is no blowing bubbles. For what purpose? It has no purpose but fun, and that is something that in my country you don't see very often. I mean just in the grocery store, for anybody to have for no reason. I wanted to remind myself to have fun just every day for no reason." He hung his head. "Do you think I am a terrible person?"

Maryka's heart did an incredible thing then. It opened up like the loving arms of the Mother Goddess and embraced the entire world. And she was indelibly in love with Dïm for giving her that gift.

Which is not to say that life with a childlike adult is always fun and games. Because there is also the tendency toward thinking only of self, a level of existing that precedes the more highly evolved quality of concern for all beings. Dïm was almost always able to charm and twinkle his way out of being the one responsible for anything to do with money, paperwork, licensing, and in general pesky things that interfere with Peace and Harmony.

He had, however, made the effort and gotten his driver's license after they ran out of college for a lifestyle and moved into the B frame to begin life as grownups. It was just too inconvenient on this island not to have transportation at hand all the time. Which was also the reason he always made sure to maintain good relations with Hank, the tenant at the other end of the property. Leni's boyfriend, he supposed, although their arrangement seemed murky to Dïm, who liked things to be more black and white (a contradiction, he was aware, with his general philosophy about life—he needed to work on that). Hank was an auto mechanic, and he had been known to freely loan out any vehicle he might have in his temporary possession if a need arose within what he called his family. If the customers who were the actual owners of the cars in question ever saw them out on the road, they either didn't notice (how many dark green Subaru's are on this island anyway?) or they were themselves loose-knit enough to shrug it off. There are places in the world, and the Northwest is one, where a cloak of aboriginal afterglow sits lightly upon the shoulders of some in modern life, reminding them that the concept of private property is a new kid on the block.

Of course the other thing Dïm did keep up with was his immigration status. Since he had long since ceased being a student, he had needed to find more and different ways of extending his visa. Naturally the coveted green card was his goal, something Dïm's own mother was still in the dark about—she thought he had every intention of repatriating even though she knew about Maryka. In Dïm's mind the most obvious and practical way to achieve citizenship status was to marry Maryka, and to that end he devoted himself entirely. To him it was like a dream—not only had he found a way to become an American (an AMERICAN!), but it was going to be with someone he worshipped and adored. And, miracle of all miracles, she loved him back! (Her name even rhymed with America, indeed almost WAS America!)

But Maryka had so far not consented to marrying Dïm, which he could not understand. She professed to love him deeply and wholly, and they got along really well, he thought. He suspected Leni of interfering with his hopes and dreams by discouraging her daughter from marrying so young (although where Dïm came from, 25 was an old maid) or possibly ever. Leni seemed to be completely soured on the whole idea of marriage. Maryka was very different from her mother but they were close nonetheless. It came of being a team, just the two of them against the world, so to speak, which is how Maryka had presented it to him as they unfolded their life stories to each other. Leni had pretty much renounced a life of anything but motherhood once that became her lot. And she scrapped every day for Maryka's well-being. Maryka knew to her core that she was loved absolutely and unconditionally. And that secure and permanent connection to the mother ship had produced in her a profound serenity about all of life. Maryka was one of the most easy-going people Dïm had ever encountered. She simply was not in a hurry.

So Dïm felt sure that it was mostly Leni's influence that was holding Maryka back from consenting to be his bride. But he also felt confident that if he persevered he would win, and then he planned to act rather surprised when telling his mother that he would not be returning to Pakistan after all because he was getting married to an American. And then his dream would be achieved and he would live happily ever after. Well sure, he realized that was a fantasy, but the reality would be enough. He would invite his parents to the wedding; it would be beautiful and they would be happy for him.

* *

Boris and Halana

Boris Petrovsky and his wife Halana Bukhari were perplexed and a little worried about Dïm's extended stay in America. Whenever they talked with him on the phone, which was not too often—usually they e-mailed (a new technology that Halana had access to through her government position)—he seemed confident and happy but a little short on specifics. Boris was lacking the typical Russian father's authoritarianism and tended to let things ride without questioning them. But this had gone on too long; Boris was nervous about his own immigration status, which made him especially anxious that his son's status remain unblemished. Pakistani citizenship law denied any dual citizenship, so Boris would have had to renounce his Russian citizenship to become an official Pakistani (an act that he would gladly perform but alas the other party—Russia—was not so willing). Consequently he had been living with the slightly tenuous status of an illegal allowed to stay only because of marriage to a natural born. He had been employed as a laborer for all these years because they were able to live off his wife's fairly decent salary in the governmental office she was attached to. His wages they put away for savings.

Boris figured it was time to use some of that savings. Halana had some vacation time coming to her, and they had booked a trip to America to meet this girl Dïm was so in love with. They hoped maybe they could give the situation a little nudge to get it unstuck, and then Dïm would bring her back to Pakistan with him. They had planned the trip to include Pakistani Independence Day, August 14, a Wednesday this year, which afforded them an extra day off. Their itinerary was to arrive on Friday, stay the weekend, and then travel in the region, maybe go on up to Vancouver if they felt like it. Neither of them had been to North America before but they knew plenty of people who had and they were excited to be finally joining those ranks. The really exciting part of the trip was that it was a surprise! They had not told Dïm they were coming! They had done all the research on just how they would need to get there—all the forms of transportation they would need to take, all the cities they would have layovers in, everything except exactly how to get from the airport to the ferry dock and across the water to this island, and then to where he lived once on the island. The island was a vague, undefined mass in their minds—they had no idea how big it was or what kind of facilities were available. However, they had decided to be adventurous and bold and trust in Allah that all would work out well, or, as Dïm would have said with his new knowledge of American slang if he had been in on the planning, "Just wing it."

This proved to be a prescient decision. The shortest and cheapest flight they could get (37 hours at best) went from Peshawar to Bahrain (six and a half hour layover) to Paris (five hour 50 minute layover "often delayed by 30+ minutes") to Chicago (two hour 20 minute layover) to Seattle. Arrival time was 7:52 pm. The problem had been the Paris to Chicago flight. The "30+ minutes" it was often delayed by turned into three hours due to weather over the city. They landed in Chicago after their Seattle connection had left, and there were no more flights to Seattle that night. The next best thing the airline could do for them was to route them to San Francisco, where they might be able to catch a connecting flight to Seattle. Boris and Halana's adventurous spirit was starting to wear thin after 28 hours of flying and hanging out in airports. They had read all the magazines in the newsstands and drunk gallons of coffee, but they agreed to fly to San Francisco in lieu of spending the night at O'Hare International.

By the time they arrived at SFO it was after midnight and there were no more flights to Seattle until the morning. A long tired line snaked around the customer service desk area where there were two slow agents assigning people to hotels for what was left of the night, compliments of the airline whose tardiness had caused the missed connections. One guy in the line was quite drunk and caused all kinds of rude commotion, yelling at the agents to hurry the f___ up, and so forth. Finally the agents called security and had him escorted away from the area. Boris and Halana were given a room at the Ocean View Embassy Suites—a fine chain of high-rise hotels with the center atrium stretching up to the very top story, a waterfall feeding a stream flowing through the lobby, and the latest in technological amenities. They could have had a complimentary breakfast if they had been able to stay that long, but they had to catch their next adventure—a 7:00 am flight to Seattle. They never even got to enjoy the view from their eleventh-floor window since it was dark when they dragged themselves down to the lobby to check out, having just checked in four and a half hours ago.

* *

Nancy Kipp

Nancy Kipp felt betrayed by the Norman Rockwell images of family, especially at Thanksgiving. Large families gathered around a table laden with the usual food, beaming, holding hands, praying. But for more years than she cared to count, her Thanksgivings had been just the two of them, she and Pete. Everyone in the government takes the day off and leaves folks alone "to be with family," but neither Nancy nor Pete had any family left, and the boys were grown, both pro football players, so they were always busy on that day. And of course Pete had to watch the games obsessively—he set up a whole other TV right next to the regular one so he could watch both games in case they were on different channels. For a few years she had valiantly made the traditional meal with all the trimmings, even making homemade rolls and the pie from a fresh pumpkin. But eventually her enthusiasm for that waned, since Pete didn't help or even seem to notice, really. They went out for dinner after that.

But last Thanksgiving Nancy had up and done something bold and different all on her own. She volunteered to help serve the Thanksgiving dinner at a homeless shelter. There was one not too far from their home in the hills outside of Santa Cruz. Of course the paparazzi came and there was some nice publicity, but that's not the reason she did it. She just knew she needed to get out. Outside, outside of herself. Do something completely different and see if it changes your perspective. When she was a freshman in college, the girl across the hall in the dorm used to occasionally stand on top of her desk, just stand there, and look around. She said it gave her another perspective. Nancy always remembered that.

And it did. Change her perspective. She saw all those many people who also were not living the Norman Rockwell Thanksgiving, possibly never had in their lives. Or possibly had for a long time, and now what had happened? Things can change in the blink of an eye, she realized.

So this year, even though it was only August, she was already thinking of what they could do for Thanksgiving that would be really different. She wanted Pete to do whatever it was with her this time, and who knows? Maybe it would become some new sort of tradition with them. Of course, there was the problem of him insisting on watching football. That might be tricky to integrate with a getaway, but she was thinking of some rustic lodge/spa type place, which would ideally have TV as well. She was keeping her eyes open here in Washington, since they had pretty much done all the California things over the years, and thus it was that on the ferry over to the Republican picnic that morning, she went upstairs to the passenger deck to wander around and discovered a huge rack of brochures for various tourist attractions around the Puget Sound. She came down when it was time to debark, her pocketbook stuffed with glossy, full-color flyers announcing whale watching tours, hundred-year-old inns featuring homemade loganberry jam events, alpaca farm stays that included shearing (optional) and spinning demonstrations, sheepdog trials, pumpkin pie bake-offs, and an energy vortex where intersecting ley lines create strange vibrational effects. All of those sounded interesting, she thought.

* *

Leni's Sidewalk Sale

One of the many things Leni wished for a do-over on was how she had taken care of her mother. Mary Kay had been a very good mother to her, and in ways that Leni was still discovering. She was, for one thing, the epitome of a genteel southern lady. Raised in Alabama, the daughter of a cotton farmer, she had married her one great love, a pilot in the U.S. Army Air Forces, which would after the war become the United States Air Force. They were old for a bride and groom, since they had waited 'til the war was over to marry. He was 40 and she was 30 when they tied the knot, and he brought his bride to the Northwest to settle down as he made a career with a national aircraft manufacturer. Leni was born in 1946. Douglas proved to be a steadfast husband and breadwinner, and he and his little family made steady progress up the ladder to the American Dream. They did not have the 2.5 children the Dream dictates, as Mary Kay suffered four miscarriages after Leni's birth, and so Leni became the sole recipient of all of her parents' love and concern. At some point, they relocated to the island, because Douglas and Mary Kay both preferred to have more land around them. He commuted to work by ferry and on the weekends worked in the garden and played golf. She started the little ceramics shop sort of as a hobby, since they didn't really need the money. It gave her something to do once Leni got into high school. They were looking forward to a comfortable retirement when, at 62, on the very first day of said retirement, Douglas dropped dead of a heart attack.

It was shortly after that that Leni discovered she was pregnant. So she came home from college, because her mother needed her and she needed her mother. Mary Kay, already overcome with grief, apparently had no energy to rail against her only daughter for becoming an unwed mother. When Leni revealed her secret, Mary Kay simply stared at her for an eternity, as if assessing the situation from every angle, then nodded once and said, "Well let's get on with it then," in that stately southern accent of hers. With the life insurance money, Leni was able to purchase the cheap five-acre lot with the A frame and start her own family life, though minus the father. The less said about him the better, in Leni's opinion. Most people were too polite to ask, but of course there are always busybodies who think it is their business to know everything. They soon learned not to ask, though, because no answers were forthcoming.

Mary Kay was there for Leni and Maryka at every turn. She made dinners for them frequently, had them over to her place often for movie nights with popcorn, and paid for Maryka's swim lessons. gymnastics classes, ballet classes, braces, and school yearbooks. Mary Kay was the very definition of the word generous, but she was also gracious about it, never holding it over Leni's head or making herself out to be some sort of martyr. In fact, she seemed to enjoy it immensely.

What Leni wished she had done when she learned of her mother's diagnosis of brain cancer was bring Mary Kay to live with her in the A frame. What she actually did was a lot of paperwork and finagling to get a spot in the local nursing home, where Mary Kay lived out her remaining months in confusion and loneliness. Sure, Leni visited her every day, sometimes with Maryka in tow, even Hank once in a while, but for the bulk of every day Mary Kay was just one of the vacant-eyed, spoonfed souls biding their time. Brain cancer—a kind that recurs 100% of the time after surgical removal and steals the self, the ability to string words together or even remember words for the world's wondrous creations.

Leni added this great sin to the weighty burden of all the others she carried in her heart. Her greatest fear and suspicion was that she, Leni, was not worthy of being Mary Kay's daughter, that she was not even marginally in the same ballpark as her mother when it came to soul-sweet righteousness.

Which is why she decided totally on the spur of the moment when she got up to the ceramics shop that Saturday (Glazy Dayz was its name, chosen by Mary Kay and somehow Leni was never able to bring herself to change it to something more . . . je ne sais quoi) to try and make this sidewalk sale something memorable. As a tribute to Mary Kay, a tribute to good motherness, or conceivably Leni had a spark of businesswoman in her after all.

She had three cases of greenware statuary in the back room of the shop that she had ordered rather inadvertently, through not paying attention to details on an invoice, and this could be the perfect solution to that little problem. They were Jerry Garcia bobblehead dolls. They sort of accidentally got ordered back in April, when Leni noticed an article in the paper about how the last of Jerry Garcia's ashes had been strewn on the Ganges River in India. That made her remember something she had seen in one of her greenware catalogues about some special Grateful Dead merchandise that was made with a tiny bit of ash from the icon himself. She thought she might try one or two of those items, just to see—I mean Deadheads were everywhere, right?—so she ordered a dozen Jerry Garcia head pins, a dozen mugs with the band, and a dozen freestanding dancing bears. The bobbleheads were a bonus offer that she somehow neglected to decline on the order form, so she ended up with a lot of Grateful Dead merchandise that so far had not generated any interest at all.

Leni's spur of the moment decision was to give away the bobbleheads! She had one that she had painted up just for fun to show; she would offer them for free but then the customer would need to purchase the glazes and brushes to paint it, and also pay for the firing of it. An age-old marketing trick but one that apparently worked enough of the time to make it worthwhile.

Hank had followed her to town and was all "tanked up and ready to go," which meant he had drunk his fill of strong coffee and needed to do some physical labor to work off the energy that was sparking off him. There were tables to be carried outside, and the three boxes of bobbleheads, along with lots of other greenware items that Leni had decided to offer at blowout prices. But Leni had perceived a problem with the plan—her shop was on one of the two side streets that ran east and west, whereas the main highway through town was north/south. What's more, her side street, although the post office was on it, contained less popular businesses—those that perhaps no one even knew existed, such as a company that dealt in table linens but not with the general public, and a small escrow firm. In fact if anyone in the town had been asked to name the businesses that abutted Glazy Dayz, they would not have been able to name one, and there certainly would be no sales of any kind there. So Leni knew she would have to do something radical to attract attention to her sale. She was the proud owner of a poster from the one Grateful Dead concert she had attended, featuring Jerry Garcia looking very like Maharishi Mahesh Yogi. This she mounted on a sandwich board she found in the back room, and painted below it a giant arrow pointing to the right. She pondered a minute over where she should place her only advertisement, and then opted for the corner of the main street by the movie theater, with the poster facing southbound traffic. At the last minute she painted the other side with the words "Jerry Garcia" and an arrow pointing left, for the benefit of northbound cars. She added a little impromptu design in bright psychedelic colors she found also in the back room.

The paint was still wet as she placed the sign on the sidewalk, just as a stream of ferry traffic was approaching from the north. There was a long line of cars, what with the Republican picnic, the WAAOW fair, Dog Days, and other summertime small town Saturday hubbub. As Leni stood back to admire her sign, a black stretch limo with American flags fluttering on each side passed the corner, and a woman's face suddenly appeared at the window; though Leni couldn't see through the tinted glass well enough to catch her expression, just for a second she felt a spark of connection pass between them.

* *

Pete and Nancy Arrive at the Picnic

Pete Kipp was also staring out the window during the ride from the ferry to the picnic, noticing that the house numbers on the mailboxes were five digits. He allowed himself to indulge in his favorite mental activity when in an area where addresses had five digits—transcribing the number into a little tune phrase, according each number its pitch in the scale. He had many of these tune phrases stored in his memory associated with the family who had lived in the house with that number. The Andersons' was CDCFG, a thoroughly pleasant little phrase, perfect for a thoroughly pleasant family, the family of his best friend growing up. Very hummable. Pete would often hum the little tunes in his memory, to the annoyance of Nancy, who complained that she just wished they were real songs. He had tried to explain to her the logical beauty of the mathematics of music, but she wasn't that interested.

If Pete hadn't gone into football he probably would have majored in music. Luckily, he was a quarterback, so his hands were always protected and he could still play the piano, which Nancy loved. But he really loved the theory of it, and even the notation. He had a logical bent, and a good head for numbers. As the car turned into the estate where the picnic was being held, Pete noted with secret irritation that the number included a zero. Zeroes were the only problem with turning house numbers into tune phrases, since there is no note assigned to the zero spot in the scale. For those, he just always put in a rest—an absence to mark that place. The number of the estate was 12011, which made for a very boring, humdrum little tune: CD_CC. Not nearly grand enough for the expanse of grandiosity Pete was about to enter.

As the massive gate swung open and the limo eased between wide arms of a lavish stone entrance welcoming them to Emerald Valley Ranch, a stunning panorama revealed itself: 525 acres of nature dressed up, spit and polished to perfection, with a three-acre lake basking in the gaze of Mt. Rainier; six different bridges; water features of every kind including a waterfall; a PGA quality driving range and putting green; pastures housing prize-winning Black Angus cattle; 3,000 evergreen and flowering trees laid out and tended by a full-time arborist; and an airstrip for light aircraft as well as a licensed helipad complete with helicopter. Even the air felt different here, somehow perfumed not with the smell of manure, or diesel fuel from all the equipment needed to maintain the place, but a heady fresh-smelling fragrance.

"Pretty nice, eh?" remarked Sam, their driver. Pete nodded. He was impressed.

"It really is nice for an out-of-the-way place like this island. As good as anything I've seen in California really," Pete replied, unconsciously allowing his California chauvinism to show.

Pete and Nancy were greeted warmly by the host himself, the creator of this paradise on earth, a billionaire businessman headquartered in Seattle but with tendrils reaching to the ends of the earth. They were shuttled by a golf cart to the picnic grounds, where a stage had been erected for the speakers and entertainment. There were twenty long tables laid out with enough food for Stalin's army, and three (!) portable bars ready and able to provide whatever libation one could desire, plus waiters circulating with trays of champagne. Well, this was not like any picnic Pete had ever attended. He glanced at Nancy with one slightly raised eyebrow. She responded the same way.

* *

Leni’s Shower

One of the reasons Leni allowed Hank to talk her into staying over occasionally was that she got to use his shower. Not that there was anything that great about it—a tiny bathroom in a camper trailer was nothing to get excited about. No, the real reason was that Leni was afraid to use her shower. Which was really too bad because it was a work of art.

Back in the days when Leni was just taking over the ceramics shop and putting in long hours there with a baby, she had created and completed a project of her own. She’d painted enough 4” square tiles to make a shower surround and crafted it as a mural. A trompe l’oeil really, as if you were looking out a big French window at a pastoral scene filled with light and trees and birds and clouds. She was actually quite talented and it was not a bad trompe l’oeil for an amateur painter. Soaking in the tub was a pleasure; guests oohed and aahed over it. It was the best feature in her house.

One detail she thought of when creating the bathroom was to put two soap dishes in—one at chest level if you were standing up showering and the other down low in case you were sitting in the bathtub. Well, something had happened (Leni never did figure out exactly who was responsible for this) and the lower soap dish broke away from the wall, leaving a gaping hole. Things don't always get fixed in a timely manner, and now it had been two or possibly three years that a square of heavy plastic taped to the wall with duct tape had been covering the hole left by the soap dish. Of course water has a way of finding its way in to protected spaces, and so it came to pass that one day Leni really looked at the situation and noticed that there was standing water behind the plastic. Then she noticed that some of the tiles around the shower control knob seemed to be slightly concave. She pressed on the wall ever so lightly and was horrified to feel a squishiness behind the tile—it gave in to her touch. Ever since that day, she had been very cautious when showering to not lean against the wall or even touch it. She was plagued with visions of the wet rock behind the tiles having soaked up two (three?) years of water and transferred the water to the studs behind the rock, which would now be rotten. Any day now, thought Leni, the whole thing was bound to just fall in upon itself, bringing who knows what all destruction with it.

* *

Dïm at the WAAOW Fair

Dïm sat cross-legged on the ground, surrounded by pots of colored sand, small bowls of seeds, and a bucket of various bright flowers in water, so as to remain as fresh as possible until their petals were plucked off and added to the sand mandala he was making. The sun was crawling up the sky, promising a warm but not stifling afternoon, so he thought the perishable elements would last fairly well. Of course the flower petals and seeds were not traditional in sand mandalas at all, and of course you couldn't make one in just one day, but Dïm had gone with a casual approach and was only loosely following protocol for the mandala. Basically he was just making a nice design on the ground. He had borrowed a tent from a friend, because wind, even a small breeze, was deadly to a sand mandala, and up here on the ridge it was almost always blowing.

He did have his compass and a protractor to make exact geometric forms, and his brushes and funnels for precise sand placement. He had started a pattern with some white, green, and blue sand but now he wanted to add red, which he was waiting for Maryka to bring to him, as he had gone off without it. So he decided to stretch his legs and wander around to see what else was going on.

Surprisingly, for a laid-back contingent of folks on a laid-back island, there was a lot of hustle and bustle. There were people setting up tents for food vendors (nut and seed bars, vegetable juices, and stir-fry rice and beans with salad) and musicians setting up the stage for the various bands that would be playing all day (heavy on the reggae). There was the booth for psychic readings, next to it was one for art in forms of sacred geometry, then one over there for jewelry made with crystals and other precious minerals. "The Natural Philosopher" had a booth full of tie-dyed clothing and also incredibly beautiful laminated posters such as The Music Mandala, which looked like the color wheel only it was called "Circle of Fifths." The circles of color were notes of the scale, and a secondary wheel of smaller circles of color had different notes. There was not a blank inch of space in between the color/note circles, but various mysterious symbols, and technical musical terminology such as "tonic" and "super-tonic," "dominant," and "submediant." In the upper left-hand corner was a quote from Oscar Wilde:

"It is said that passion makes one think in a circle."

Dïm found that fascinating. The Natural Philosopher had tie-dyed T-shirts with color patterns of musical chords, the pattern made by the frequencies of the notes, using an invention he came up with called a Harmonochord. Another poster was mostly writing, with topics such as "The Logic of Beauty—Music as Ecology," and "Scaling the Heights—the Heliacal Rainbow." It was all very intriguing.

Then there were those with no booth but just a sign, such as the lady whose mission in life was to promote laughter as healing—she was inviting you to share jokes with her. There was face painting for the kids, and drawing, and someone was attempting to get a Slip 'n Slide in place but others were looking skeptical about the mess that would create with the resulting mud, and also there was the issue of wasting water.

Fair-goers were already in attendance—those hard-core enthusiasts who brought camping gear and were prepared to hang out all day and night; more casual participants were beginning to drift in around the edges, some early bird garage-salers who just came by to look, and the usual assortment of islanders who could be seen at events like this. The young woman with purple hair and a gauzy lingerie slip-thing, and then chunky Doc Martins on her feet; the old guy with the white beard down to his waist playing a didgeridoo; Dolly, the sturdy sensible-looking woman with a ponytail and horn-rimmed glasses who rode her no-speed bicycle everywhere she went.

Ah—finally—there came Maryka, lugging the heavy bucket of sand. He hailed her and walked back with her to his mandala tent but did not take the bucket from her. Maryka found that this irked her no end. Although she had no real father figure to draw on, she had Hank, whom she had known all her life and watched as he performed one chivalrous thing after another for Leni, who never seemed to Maryka grateful enough. She always thought to herself that if she ever got a man that good, she would be more appreciative. Well, it appeared that perhaps she wouldn't have to worry about that.

She hung around Dïm's tent for a while watching him work on the mandala and chatting about how she had had to borrow Leni's car again because theirs was being persnickety, and how Leni was fuming about the Dog Days sale and the Republican picnic. Dïm paid little attention to these things, as he considered them too mundane to be worthy of his interest. A few people stopped by and that was when he really came to life and was suddenly animated and enthusiastic about showing them how he used the tools to make precise forms, and sometimes even letting them try it. Maryka smiled to herself at his un-self-conscious eagerness to share, tapped him on the shoulder, and said she would be back later.

* *

Maryka at the Fair

Maryka walked around for a little while and looked at all the booths. She constantly had in the back of her mind the possibility of finding something fun for her class to do. Maryka was the pre-kindergarten teacher at a very popular preschool on the island. She was able to use all of her creative and artistic sensibilities with this job and had the freedom to do so. She was always coming up with unusual projects and ideas for those kids. Even though it was only part-time and didn't pay that much, it was rather a 24/7 job, because her mind was never far from it.

But she found nothing that inspired her in that way at the WAAOW fair. She began to think of going up to town, to the sidewalk sales, and also to stop in at the shop and say something supportive of Leni, see how she was doing. Maryka knew nothing of Leni's whole Grateful Dead plan. She bought a vegetarian burrito and started hiking back to where she had parked—almost half a mile down the road. She amused herself by keeping count of all the colorful hippie vehicles—old beater pickups, vans plastered with bumper stickers, cars with rainbow glitter on every inch—on the north side vs. all the Lincoln Towncars and Cadillacs on the south. But then she came in view of the 30-acre pasture belonging to the billionaire businessman, which was, amazingly, today a shared parking lot for both big events—the WAAOW fair and the Republican picnic, and she gave up trying to count. She arrived at her white Toyota—rather Leni's white Toyota, which she had borrowed (she almost thought of it as hers, she borrowed it so frequently), got in, and sat there for a few minutes while she considered what the rest of her day should be until she went back to the fair later for the music. She didn't really want to hang out there all day. She decided to go to town and check in at the shop at least, then see what developed. Maybe she would just go home for a while and relax by herself. That sounded lovely actually; she had been feeling tired lately.

* *

The Dead Save the Day

Town was actually buzzing with activity this Saturday. Leni had not realized what a big deal it was going to be. There was even a short parade during which the main street was closed off to cars, so people were shuttling off onto the side streets. Between that and the tantalizing smell of grilling hot dogs (free!) across the street in the supermarket parking lot, Leni's display attracted more people than she had ever imagined it would. Or rather it just happened to be on their way to somewhere else, and it looked interesting, so they stopped to look. Hank had helped put out all the tables she had, and all the merchandise she hoped to get rid of, including the Grateful Dead bobbleheads, mugs, pins, and dancing bears. Leni had told Hank about the Dead stuff a few days ago, and he had thoughtfully added a little touch which doubled the attention-getting factor—he had brought a CD player and two Grateful Dead CD's, hooked up a speaker, and bam! Toe-tapping, feel-good music blasting forth from Glazy Dayz's open door. Leni began to feel the old buzz of those days, and started being real friendly with people, and consequently had made a few new friends and customers too.

It helped that one other thing happening that very same weekend as everything else was Wildisle—a huge free festival for the arts of all kinds—just show up and camp out there and do art for free. Sing, dance, transform the woods into a magical wonderland, make puppets, tell stories, write scripts, build installations, whatever. Actually this lasts for a month but the culmination weekend was especially big and festive and included a parade the next day (Sunday). Anyway, some of those folks had drifted by and one had been seized with the inspiration to build a giant Jerry Garcia papier-mache puppet head, and insisted that they each should get a mug to commemorate this feat. Being very enthusiastic and spontaneous (and perhaps a little high), they trooped in right then and there and started applying the glazes they needed to bring their mugs to life. They got slightly carried away with everything and ended up snapping up most of the Grateful Dead merchandise, and having a glazing marathon. It was all very jolly. Leni was enjoying herself, but Hank seemed restless. He offered to go get Leni a hot dog as an excuse to get out of there. But then of course he was back with the hot dog. Among all those . . . those art people. I mean, it's fine, thought Hank, to be able . . . to have the luxury of creating ephemeral whimsical things. He himself had always felt the need to just try and fix the stuff that was already here. He found he had no idea what to say to them.

Well he could just leave, of course. It wasn't his business after all. Leni had always made it perfectly clear that she didn't need his help with her business decision-wise, only when the need for brawny shoulders arose. She wouldn't even notice if he left, probably. Besides, Hank was feeling an urge to get home—an intuition perhaps. Hank often had intuitions, despite a common misconception that intuition is the exclusive domain of women; and what's more, he had the good sense to pay attention to them.

Just as he was preparing to exit the room, he caught Leni's eye and she waved a heartfelt thank you and blew him a kiss. "I'll see you later" he mouthed and signaled, and she nodded. He dipped his head and winked at her, and called out, "You could take me out to dinner with your profits from today!" Leni licked her lips and wrinkled her nose, in that order, a thing that Hank found impossible to interpret. So he turned and escaped to his truck.

* *

Boris and Halana's Journey Continues

Boris and Halana both felt as if they were moving through molasses, they were that tired. After arriving in Seattle by 9:00 am, they realized the hardest part of their journey was ahead of them. This is when the broad strokes end and the detail work begins. They had figured out every step as far as the nearest big city, but this island, and how to get there from the airport, and then how to find the house where Dïm lived (which they had an address for)—these were all unknown. They were going to have to throw themselves on the mercy of others—they were going to have to ask for help from total strangers, and now they were so tired they were barely coherent, never mind the language barrier problem. Sure, Boris had had the required five years of English as a young student, where the teacher was not a native speaker and the motivation of the learners was totally absent, but he hadn't spoken it at all in his real life for all these years. Halana had been fortunate to be one of a tiny fraction of girls who actually got to attend a government school that had electricity (though no toilets or qualified teachers), in a system that was universally acknowledged to be an unqualified failure in every single aspect. While she had been able to grasp basic strategies despite all that, still she never had the opportunity to really learn English, and in fact only used Urdu in her life (which Boris had had to learn). But later, raising Dïm, Pakistani education got a little better, at least for a boy, and before it was Islamized; English references began to be noticeable, and she picked it up enough to understand it, but not to speak it more than very haltingly. So neither one's English was that great under favorable circumstances, but now? Boris seriously felt that the best approach might be to go with the poor helpless immigrant look, and make a sign to hang around their necks that just said the name of the island, and then underneath that the word "Help?" question mark.

But Halana was stalwart. You don't work in the bowels of a feudal family's government fighting ruthlessly to retain power by being faint of heart. She insisted she would be fine after a cup of good Seattle espresso and a brief rest in a comfy chair during which she planned to think her way through this. And she was. It wasn't that hard really to find a shuttle bus to the ferry dock. Boris was so proud of her, the way she always figured out what to do. She knew this and did not mention to him that she had not gotten as far as what to do once they got to the other side. That was something she could not visualize. However, she was prepared to offer someone money.

As it turned out, the sight of two bone-weary foreign travelers trudging onto the ferry with their luggage in tow was more than a certain islander could bear to watch. Did they even know there was an elevator they could use to go upstairs and sit down for the ride? Most likely they did not. As the cars poured onto the car deck on this busiest of Saturdays, Geraldine made a dash for the small space where Boris and Halana were standing forlornly at the foot of the stairs with their suitcases, no doubt preparing themselves for hoisting their heavy bags up the narrow two-story flight of steps.

"Hello!" she called, cutting between vehicles packed three lanes deep. Boris and Halana looked around to see whom she might be speaking to, but they were the only ones there. They nodded uncertainly. Was she going to tell them they could not take luggage upstairs? She didn't look like an official ferry person, but then everything here was new to them.

"It looks like you could use some help," she said brightly. Well she looks friendly, thought Halana as she smiled tentatively. Was this some trick to provide a service and charge lots of money? "May I offer you a ride in my car? You look exhausted, and it's a steep walk up the hill once we get to the island. I'd be happy to take you to where you're going. Oh but no doubt someone is picking you up."

Halana admitted, shaking her head, that no one was picking them up, and that they were here on a surprise visit to see their son—"son" was the one word Halana knew to say, and when combined with a surprised look, conveyed all the meaning necessary. Geraldine's eyes widened. She was a perky seventy-something woman with still-red hair who was an activist in many a good cause but particularly pet rescue. This couple put her in mind of a pair of animals in need of a home and a good meal, and her protective instincts kicked in.

"Please allow me to help by giving you a ride to your destination," she said in formal English, as this seemed to be the kind of speech they might be most familiar with. Halana felt almost giddy with relief and gratitude that this last and hardest leg of the journey had been flooded with grace, and she could hardly stop the tears from streaming down her face or her smile from breaking wide open. They threaded their way carefully through the cars, following Geraldine to her minivan, where she heaved their bags into the back and helped them up into the seat. Boris showed her the piece of paper where Dïm's address was written down, the last entry on an itinerary two pages in length and by this time very smudged and wrinkled. Geraldine mentally raised her eyebrows but said only that she thought she knew where this was—it was hardly even out of her way—and would be happy to take them there.

In fact it was very much out of her way, being at the end of a very long and rutted dirt road, admittedly not very far from the main highway as the crow flies, but as the car drives, about ten minutes of knowing where to follow the arterial and where to turn off and which way to swerve to avoid the worst potholes. But islanders are not fazed by these things, and so Geraldine was able to discharge her two world travelers with good humor and aplomb, humbly shaking off their profuse thanks and offers of payment.

Geraldine drove off, leaving Boris and Halana to look around at the scene they found themselves in. They had not expected there to be two houses here. Which one was Dïm's? One was a two-story A-frame log-style house, and the other was something that looked like it had started life as a chicken coop perhaps. Or a shop. The sun was beating down on them, and Boris was just about to take the initiative of looking in the window of the low house when the sound of another car approaching stopped him. It was Hank's pickup, knowing exactly how to weave expertly around the ruts so as to sound completely smooth. They were, then, a tiny bit surprised to see a well-used faded red truck with a few dents pull up to within feet of where they stood—a truck like that at home would never sound so good.

Hank was good at taking things in stride. It was one of his best qualities, and he was a man of many good qualities. So when his intuition led him to come home at that time to find a lost-looking Pakistani couple with luggage in his driveway, he may have mildly wondered "what the hell" in his mind, but what his body did was jump out of the truck in a very friendly manner with his handshake arm extended, a smile on his face, and a definite-sounding "Hello!"

And with that attitude things can progress without too many problems. As soon as they said the name Dïm, Hank grasped the basic situation and realized the only decent thing to do would be to invite them in to his place for a cup of tea perhaps. He explained that Dïm was at the fair today, along with half the island it seemed like. Then he got the idea that he should offer to take them up there to see Dïm, but only if they allowed him to provide them some rest or refreshment at his place first. They agreed, assuming his place was one of the two they were looking at. Leaving their luggage where it was, he led them farther up the dirt driveway, beyond the houses and through a copse of trees to another clearing, where a canvas shelter shaded a mechanic's workspace, then farther yet through another stand of trees and finally to the clearing where stood his adorable little Airstream trailer. Halana thought she might collapse before they got there, but again, her stamina won out.

They half staggered in the front door, gratefully taking note of the cleanliness of it all. Hank sat them down on his little couch and proceeded to scurry around his tidy kitchen boiling water for tea. Halana sank back against the pillowy cushion and began to unclench. When Hank asked about their journey, Boris filled him in as best he could with the language he had, and the ticket stubs from their various flights. Hank had no idea what time it was for them, but he noticed it was lunchtime for him, and so politely offered them some lunch as well, which they accepted with grace. He stood in the middle of the kitchen wondering what he possibly could have in his tiny pantry that he might serve them. Finally he decided to ask if they liked tuna fish salad, because he could whip that up in the blink of an eye. But when he went around the corner back to the living room they were both sound asleep.

* *

Hank in a Quandary

Hank didn't know what to do at that point. He felt he shouldn't leave them alone, but then he also felt he should leave them alone. It was awkward, having them in his living room like that. Then he had what he thought was a fairly decent idea—he would get them set up in Leni's house. Obviously that was going to have to be the ultimate plan anyway, because the B frame could not accommodate guests, and Leni's house had lots of rooms. They should definitely not stay with him, because he and Dïm barely knew each other, not to mention the Airstream could not accommodate guests either. So Leni's was the obvious and really the only choice—she could not disagree with that. These people had had an arduous time getting here for God's sake.

So he went down to the A frame and collected all their luggage (one large bag apiece and one carry-on apiece) and hauled it inside. He decided to put them in the upstairs guest room, the nicest one and the cleanest. Leni lived in the upstairs herself and had rather taken to storing things downstairs—another reason Hank put them upstairs. Leni was not the most conscientious housekeeper, and too, she had a hard time throwing things out. She was not a hoarder, or even close to that, but the place could have used a thorough decluttering and cleaning. For one thing, she still had all of Mary Kay's things—those were crammed into one extra room downstairs, including Mary Kay's ashes, which were in a vase on a shelf in the closet.

He made sure that the bed had clean sheets, which it did. He checked in the bathroom to make sure there were clean towels and other linens in the closet. There were. He glanced at the tub. Oh yeah—there was that tilework that needed fixing. He vaguely recalled that Leni had told him about that some time ago. She hadn't specifically asked him to fix it, but he knew that they both considered him to be the unofficial handyman on the property. Hmm . . . well he would have to get to that soon. Probably not life-threatening, he thought, amused with himself for that.

Hank momentarily considered the odd fact that he was just now aware of, the fact that it was mostly Leni coming to his place when they spent time together. Why were they never here? And when he was here, often it was in a handyman capacity. Strange. They were in this weird dance together, he reflected, for 25 years now—how had that much time passed really? What were they doing? Were they "together" he wondered? He suddenly felt that it was an affair based solely on the whims of one person—her.

He recalled the day he met her—it was a time of turmoil for the family. Leni's father had just dropped dead and she had come home from college all around the same time. After the dust settled, she ended up with this property and the business that had been her mother's. Where he came into the picture was the day of moving her out of Mary Kay's house and into the A frame. He had been on the island for a couple of years already, and had a small but loyal clientele of folks whose vehicles he maintained and repaired out of a garage he rented. He lived in the little Airstream and parked it behind the garage. To make a little money on the side, he did odd jobs involving trucks—hauling brush, dump runs, that sort of thing. Mary Kay hired him and his medium-sized moving van to transport Leni's meager belongings and childhood memories to her new dwelling, while Leni with her two-thirds of a baby in her belly looked on. Nothing about her that day set off any fireworks in him. Just another girl that doesn't know enough to keep from getting pregnant, he thought rather scornfully. From the superior age of six years her senior, he was mildly disdainful of "college students these days." He wasn't against college, but in general he thought college students slightly clueless about practical matters.

It was a couple of weeks later that Mary Kay contacted him once again. As Fate would have it, the car Leni had been using—her dad's snazzy red Buick convertible—blew a head gasket and wasn't worth fixing. Well, Leni was obviously going to need a car to live on her own, especially with a child, so did he know of anything cheap but reliable? (What did she think he was anyhow—a used car lot?) But somehow she prevailed upon him to undertake a search for a suitable vehicle for her only daughter. Of course Leni was involved in that search, as she had to approve the choice (although Mary Kay was paying for it). It came down to a little VW station wagon or a 1960 Peugeot sedan. Leni didn't figure she would have any more kids, so she opted for the sedan, and also because—French car.

It was during this interlude that Hank came to see Leni in a whole new light. She was interesting, in a prickly sort of way. She said surprising things, things that made him perk up his brain and ponder. Things like, "Ooh—that gives me the tingly head!" She said this only occasionally, and once he had asked her what she meant by that, since it seemed she was referring to a specific feeling, and he was curious as to what that was. All she could say was, "I don't know how to describe it or if I'm the only person in the world who feels it. It's really good though. It's like an orgasm in your brain. Sometimes it just comes over me, and if I'm real still but don't look directly at it and try to grasp it, it washes over me like . . . like . . . waves or something. I don't know." Hank was envious of her after that. And kind of wanted to protect her from losing that feeling, although what that meant was completely unknowable. After her baby was born, she was a little less prickly and appeared content to do nothing more with her life than be a mom. Although content was not a term anyone would use to describe Leni. More like fiercely and single-mindedly devoted to the cause of being Maryka's mother. The Peugeot, to no one's surprise, ended up needing a fair amount of work, so Hank became rather a fixture in their lives, the three generations of females.

Hank glanced at the bathroom tile once more, and again decided that now was not the time to look at it. He went downstairs and out the front door but stopped in the yard. Well, now he had a plan for the people he had just met a half hour ago, but no plan for himself. He decided to goof off and take advantage of the hammock in the shade, smoke a joint and contemplate his situation some more. He would be within hearing range of his living room for when they awoke, at which point he would serve them some lunch and then take them down to their real rooms. He guessed he should call Leni and tell her what was going on. But first the contemplation. Which took the form of more reminiscing.

When Maryka was about one year old, Hank's rented garage suddenly was put on the market and he had to find another place to live and work. Mary Kay was the one to have the brilliant idea of him moving to the rear part of Leni's five acres and paying Leni the rent. It would be a win-win situation, because Leni was still in honeymoon mode with her baby and had not really worked that much and could use the money; and it was a spacious area for Hank to fill up with cars and still have a private and lush clearing for his abode. Plus he would be so handy for fixing the car. And so it happened. When Leni saw the darling little Airstream, she was thunderstruck, and her stereotyped idea of who Hank was went out the window. She and Maryka had a sleepover there that very night. It gave her the tingly head.

Thinking back on how their "relationship" (?) developed, Hank could see that over time, he and Leni surprised each other every once in awhile, which led to deep talks, which always led to romantic encounters, and more and more familiarity, until here they were, 25 years later, in this habit of familiarity. And familial ties really. Let's face it, thought Hank, he was like a father to Maryka. At least he felt that way. But it had always been sort of on Leni's terms, he could see that now. They had never discussed their status as a couple. Hank was the sort to drift along if things were fine, without rocking the boat. He wasn't really interested in a marriage either, as he valued his independence too much. So here we are, he thought. Twenty-five years.

* *

The Republican Picnic

The picnic was a smashing success in terms of fundraising. Everyone was feeling loose and generous, thanks to the copious quantities of alcohol provided by the billionaire businessman. Pete's speech had gone over well, and there had been much glad-handing all around, which Nancy had had to participate in, pretending that she cared about these people; well of course she cared, but really she wasn't that interested in them. Whenever she could sneak a minute for herself she went off on one of the mini-tours organized by the grounds staff to show off the world-class arboretum they had created on the estate, which was stunning in its scope and elegance. She would give the billionaire businessman credit for good taste in landscaping, that's for sure, or at least the sense to hire a really good designer.

Nancy was feeling pretty chipper herself, having indulged in perhaps a bit of gluttony when the beef that had been smoking for two days was served up. That was without a doubt the best barbecue she had ever tasted. And of course she had had a never-ending flute of champagne in her hand all day, so the golf cart rides to see the estate were welcome rest.

By 2:00 in the afternoon, people were starting to drift away. That's when the billionaire businessman got the idea to offer helicopter rides over the island, to raise a little more cash. Only four people could fit in the helicopter besides the pilot, so the ride would have to be pretty short, or people would get impatient and leave. He decided to offer 15-minute rides for a mere ten bucks a person, and the response was immediate—the guests started lining up with their money at the ready. Since Pete was the guest of honor, and running for the highest office in the land, naturally he didn't have to pay, and he and Nancy got the very first ride, which they shared with the state's governor (a Democrat, but he considered it politically expedient to schmooze with every presidential candidate because, well you never know) and the chair of the state Republican Party, a no-nonsense fiscally conservative woman.

The copter lifted off noisily, as copters do, from the helipad, but the pilot was very good and the ride was smooth and not at all scary, which Nancy had thought it might be a little. They cruised first to the west and followed the coastline up to the north end, where they could see the ferries crossing between the island, the mainland, and the Olympic peninsula. From there they buzzed over to the east side and down that shoreline, skipped the adjoining island, and headed to the south end, where the view of Mt. Rainier was stunning. Nancy was surprised at how many trees there were. It was lovely but you really couldn't distinguish any landmarks or human activity. The bright blue patches in many places turned out to be tarps, and not swimming pools as Nancy had thought, but there were a few pools too. Only when they were returning to the estate, where its surprising size was evident, and impressive, and everyone in the copter was oohing and pointing out features they had missed, did Nancy happen to glance the other direction, across the street from the estate. There did seem to be a lot of activity there. Since the copter was about to land and they were not very high in altitude, Nancy could plainly see pop-up shelters, colorful flags, banners, and a stage with a band playing. She did a double take and checked to make sure it was not her own picnic, in case she was somehow disoriented, but no, there was the picnic across the road, with its own stage but no pop-up shelters. There were the three full bars and the fleet of golf carts. And the three-acre lake. The one across the street had no lake, but included some sort of water thing.

Indeed it turned out that the Slip 'n Slide issue had been resolved and it had been installed on a considerable slope that ended in a safe flat area. By this time in the afternoon, it being a hot day in August, there had been enough slipping and sliding to form a veritable mud bog at the bottom, which the little ragamuffins (that's the first word that came to Nancy's mind when she glimpsed this ever so briefly) loved even more. How they squealed with delight when they landed splat in that glorious warm brown bed, or so Nancy imagined, since nothing could be heard over the copter's engine. Nancy wondered if there were responsible adults overseeing the event, for safety's sake, and of course there would be, of course there would, but a deeply secret part of Nancy's soul wished that there would not be, and that the kids were in charge of themselves. How very Tom Sawyer/Huckleberry Finn! How thrilling to be back in an era where kids were not supervised so much. She thought of The Great Brain books, books she had loved reading to her boys, about the adventures of three brothers—true stories from the author's own family—growing up in Utah around the turn of the nineteenth century. The amazing and dangerous things that happened, and the cleverness and fearlessness, nay heedlessness, with which they took things on, and hilarious to boot. Well it was breathtaking really.

The copter landed without a hitch, the passengers climbed out, and the next ones got in. The billionaire businessman was congratulated and thanked profusely, and then, then there was a slight awkward moment, in which each person was silently wondering what to do now. Nancy felt like maybe they had been there long enough—how long were they expected to stay anyway?

She was signaling Pete with her eyes toward the exit direction, when the billionaire businessman practically grabbed Pete by his shoulder and insisted exuberantly that the two of them play a round on the three-hole golf course. Of course Pete would love nothing better, so Nancy closed her eyes, pursed her lips, nodded, and headed in the general direction of the road, though of course she did not intend to leave without Pete. She thought she could hear some music wafting in the air, and since the picnic's entertainment was over, there was nothing to block out the pleasant sounds that were calling to her. Reggae, she believed it was. Along the way she picked up another flute of champagne.

* *

Boris and Halana at the A Frame

Boris and Halana slept for two hours, the deepest of sleeps with dreams of flying and sailing and swooping and gliding and falling and being caught by the softest of clouds. When they awoke they were famished, and Hank's tuna salad was gobbled up in no time at all. He had to pull out every pickle, every bag of crispy things, every bottle of fizzy water that he had on hand, and still they looked around hopefully for more. Then their manners reoccurred to them, and they began effusively thanking Hank for his hospitality and looking toward their next move, which should be to Dïm's home, as they informed him.

Hank had to explain that the B frame was not large enough to accommodate guests, and that they would be staying with Leni, the mother of Maryka, who had the larger house. And who, when Hank had called the shop to tell her about her unexpected houseguests, had thrown a mild hissy fit over the phone. Some of her customers from Wildisle were clearly shocked at the language that came out of her mouth, for Leni was not averse to swearing. Hank had heard worse though, over the years, and so he recognized this one as a mild hissy fit. He knew that he would easily be able to make her see the light on this one—this was a no-brainer. Jeez Leni.

So he installed Boris and Halana in the upstairs guest room of the A frame, and said that he would be at their service to take them to see their son whenever they were ready. They said they would really like to "freshen up" a bit, by which they meant the longest hottest bath they could manage. He showed them the bathroom, fresh towels and all, and they oohed and aahed over the trompe l'oeil mosaic on the wall. Then Hank left them alone.

Dïm's parents lay on the double bed just staring up at the pine ceiling, reeling from the three-day trip, but actually feeling pretty good after that power nap and lunch at Hank's place. (Who was he, they wondered, and what was his role here?) Their minds wandered all over the place.

Boris looked over at his wife, still a very attractive woman at 50. He remembered how drawn to her he had been the first time he saw her in Peshawar. He had only come across the border from Afghanistan two weeks before, one of the first to do so of the hundreds who would eventually switch sides. Boris wasn't cut out for the military life. He only got to be an officer because he was smart. He had a soft heart, and never really fit in as a Russian either. He had been glad to go to war just to get away from that slut of a wife he had. The humiliation of being cuckolded and everyone in his village being aware of it was more than he knew what to do about.

Boris let his hand rest on Halana's thigh. He turned on his side and snuggled closer to her, nestling his head on her shoulder.

"Remember the first day we met?" he whispered. He felt her head nod. "At the marketplace?"

"I remember," she said. "You were about to select some vegetables that were not so fresh."

Halana had been shopping for her family when their eyes found each other over the onions. He was fending for himself, staying at a rooming house, cooking over a hotplate, and only preparing the most basic dishes. Those eyes of hers! So huge and dark, with impossibly long lashes.

"I could not believe I was looking at such a beautiful creature," he reminisced dreamily. "I wanted so badly to see the rest of you. Ha! The way we moved our eyes around at each other! How did we manage to communicate?"

He felt her smile. "Well I found your cheekbones to be very entrancing. I wanted to trace them with my fingers over and over. And your hair—so wild and willful. I wanted to bury my hands in it for hours. Somehow we managed."

She had had on the traditional headscarf, but in the clandestine, almost wordlessly arranged meetings they had after that, Boris was to learn that she was anything but traditional in her heart. A long-time devotee of Benazir Bhutto and her father, through all of their trials and tribulations, she had determinedly become one of a small minority of Pakistani women who worked outside the home. She was feeling the worldwide rise of feminism one could say. She got a lowly clerical job in a local government office, kept her eyes downcast, did excellent work beyond reproach, and bent whichever way the wind blew. Her family, though, was constantly putting pressure on her to marry, and at 25 she was feeling some yearnings of her own in that direction. A chance encounter with a handsome foreigner in the market appealed to her sense of adventure, and the rest is history, as they say. Her persistence in the workplace had paid off, Benazir Bhutto was now in office as the prime minister, and life was good. If only her son would come home with a wife, then it would be perfect.

Boris' other hand slipped down between her legs.

"Mm-mm. I'm dirty. Must wash first." She got up from the bed and, looking at Boris, unabashedly stripped off her clothes, turned, and headed for the bathroom. Boris took a deep breath and blew it out slowly. By the time he heard the shower running, he was also naked. He strode into the bathroom and pulled back the curtain. Halana was standing under the steaming spray with her eyes closed, basking in the wet flowing down her entire body. She startled and looked at Boris with wide eyes—they had never done *this* before. But it was the trip for adventure, so . . .

The illusion of standing in a shower naked in front of open French windows and looking out on a lush pastoral scene only added an extra dollop of excitement to their very erotic encounter there in that shower. Both Boris and Halana were practically delirious with passion. He was nibbling her ear and murmuring all the ways he loved loved loved her, while thrusting himself into her up against that tile wall, which their eyes told them was up against thin air. It was dizzying. The sponginess of the wall they were thrusting against was hardly noticeable and never had a chance of getting through to the left brain of either one. Halana wanted it to never end. She was completely open—her legs wrapped around Boris' torso—she had never felt so free! They were moaning and gasping so loudly, both of them, that they did not hear the creaks and groans coming from the studs and joists holding that shower together.

They most certainly did hear the loud CRACK though, that separated the tub from the wall. Boris had never moved so fast in his life, especially considering the physical situation from which he had to extricate himself. Basically he just whipped around, still holding Halana up by her butt, and leaped over the side of the tub, which had dropped lower than the floor by about nine inches, so the leap was no mean feat. In fact it was an awkward combination of scrabbling for a foothold and grabbing at towel racks. Halana was screaming her head off, showing signs of hysteria really, as Boris pulled her farther away from the rapidly sinking tub, and the collapsing floor it was taking with it. In the hall they paused and looked back through the doorway. Jagged two by fours hung out over an empty space where the tub had been; water was spurting everywhere from the pipe ripped away from its controls, and they had no idea what to do.

* * *

Hank heard the screaming from his mechanic "shop," where he had stopped to check on whether the part he had ordered for a carburetor was the right model number. His head jerked up when he heard the shrill shrieking that would not stop, and then he heard a crashing sound that made him bolt like a spooked mare down toward the A frame. He took the stairs two at a time and was at full gallop in the hall before he saw the naked, dripping couple gaping at the bathroom doorway, Halana still whimpering. He skidded to a halt and tried to look away but not before the sight of him seeing her naked caused Halana to start screaming again. He didn't know what to do. Obviously he had to take care of something fast—he could hear water spraying everywhere. He motioned to Boris to take her into the bedroom, then he peeked into what was left of the bathroom. Good God, the tub had fallen completely through the floor into the room below, which was the laundry room. The crash he had heard was the cast iron tub hitting the washer and dryer, mangling them beyond recognition. He turned and ran back down the stairs and outside to the water shut-off valve and stopped the water. What to do next?! He ran back upstairs to see if Boris and Halana were hurt. He found them wrapped in towels huddling together in the bedroom, Halana sniffling loudly and trying to get her breath under control. They were not hurt but just mightily traumatized.

Hank felt they should evacuate the house immediately. They could hear more cracks and groans and popping sounds coming from the bathroom, and he suspected that the toilet would be the next to go. Hank wasn't sure how far it might spread, this collapsing floor, so he grabbed all of their bags and motioned for them to follow him down the stairs. They were standing in front of the house, Hank looking as perplexed and upset as he ever had, and the naked Pakistani couple clinging to each other and trying to hold the towels around themselves. And that's when Maryka drove up and had her first glimpse of Dïm's parents.

* *

Awkward Moments

Instantly Maryka realized who they were. She didn't really know any other Pakistanis, and besides, it was clear that Dïm was related to this beautiful woman, even in the bedraggled state she was in at the moment. Maryka's own maternal instincts materialized that very second, and she jumped out of the car and ran to greet them, which was tricky, given their situation. She quickly shepherded them into her house, the B frame, motioned to Hank to bring their bags, and left them in privacy to get some clothes on. Returning to the front yard, she looked frantically at Hank for an explanation. He shrugged and said, "I found them right here, same as you, only they were fully dressed." And then he sketched out the basic scenario of what had happened, omitting, of course, certain details of which he was unaware. Both of them felt shaken because they had been ignorant of the extent of the water damage that Leni was worried about. She had never complained about it that much, or had she? Had they just been so self-centered that they didn't pay attention? Hank took her inside and showed her the flattened washer and dryer. Maryka groaned. They both knew that Leni was going to absolutely freak out. Suddenly there was another big crash—the toilet joined the bathtub, drenching everything below that much more. Maryka screamed and jumped back three feet, grabbing onto Hank for support. They hurried back outside, where Boris and Halana had reappeared, looking somewhat more presentable but very worried. If this was the kind of place where Dïm lived, well . . . they were prepared to kidnap him and take him home if necessary.

The four of them stood around uncertainly, each thinking his or her own thoughts. Maryka was filled with the dread of telling Leni about her bathroom and laundry room, and Hank was ruefully pretty certain that his Saturday night date and sleepover with Leni would not be happening, at least not in a pleasant way. Of course what Hank and Maryka did not know was that Boris and Halana felt responsible for the devastation of Leni's house. They thought that their lovemaking was so powerful that it caused the whole room to implode. They were at once embarrassed and awestruck at themselves, as well as profoundly apologetic for the destruction of Leni's property, someone they didn't even know yet. They were so filled with adrenalin from all the events of the day that Halana felt she might have a heart attack. Boris thought he might throw up.

But something had to be done, obviously, and Hank stepped up. He suggested that he take Boris and Halana to see Dïm. He could drop them off on his way to the shop to give Leni the terrible news. They eagerly agreed and even seemed to perk up a little.

"Just let me get my other car—the truck can only take one passenger," he called, already loping toward his end of the property.

Then it was just them and Maryka, awkwardly standing around, not knowing what to say to each other. Maryka valiantly tried to make small talk.

"Um, how was your trip?" she inquired hesitantly. The look they gave her was all she needed to know. "No, never mind that," she hastened to say. "We, uh, I mean, this is such a surprise—we had no idea you were coming to visit."

"It was meant to be a surprise visit," said Boris dolefully. "But not like this."

Maryka nodded. "Well, Dïm will certainly be surprised to see you." She was thinking she should go with them and show them where he was set up but when she tried to imagine the scene at the fair when Dïm set eyes on his parents, she got a queasy feeling in her stomach. What was that about, she was curious. If there was one thing that she always remembered from that psych class she took, it was to listen to the body—the body has ways of telling you something is going on. So then she thought it would be better if she wasn't there. Some things are perhaps better just between family members. She thought instead she might stay here and wait for Leni to come storming home like a raging cyclone. That would also be better just between family members, well and probably Hank, since technically he sort of was the catalyst for it happening, apparently. She was curious what had actually been the initiating event for the collapse.

So yes, she would stay here and clean her own house and try to prepare for whatever was going to happen next. "Hank will show you where Dïm's tent is," she told them just as Hank came tooling down the driveway in his Volkswagen van. They nodded and turned to climb into the van, where Hank was already waiting to help them.

"Just maybe . . . keep an eye on the place, I'm thinking," Hank said to Maryka. "You know? Until I get back and your mom comes and we can make a plan. You know, in case the whole second story comes down. I don't think it will," he added quickly, "but who knows what freak things can happen. Stay out of it, though."

Maryka nodded. She was practiced at nodding. She was a good listener—that was one of the qualities that made her a good teacher. "Okay. Yeah. I'll just see you when you get back then."

And with that Hank hopped briskly into the van and was off. He felt a chasm of not-knowing-what-to-say yawning around him like the Grand Canyon. And he felt incredibly apprehensive about telling Leni of the disaster but extremely anxious to get it over with. So many feelings churning around inside him! Hank did not often show signs of agitation—it wasn't his style and he wasn't used to it—so what he did was start whistling. That was his way. Most people hearing that would never guess he was agitated, but Leni knew.

He was whistling when he parked right in the small parking lot where Glazy Dayz had the sidewalk sale. Things had wound down—Dog Days sales were only scheduled until 2:00—and Leni was starting to clean up. She heard him whistling through his open window and her antenna went up as to why. Somehow he never whistled when he was happy; she had known him for a long time and had observed this consistently. When he was happy, he would hum. Whistling meant something was wrong.

* *

Boris and Halana at the Picnic

Hank had been so anxious and apprehensive about telling Leni everything that he rather gave Boris and Halana the short shrift. He dropped them off on the road in front of the festival site, assuming they would find their way into the WAAOW fair, assuming they knew what their son would be doing. He didn't actually point them in any particular direction, however. And since there were two equally large gatherings, one right across the street from the other, the Pakistani couple were confused. Given their extreme state of exhaustion and trauma, perhaps they were to be excused for gazing from one side to the other, from the Cadillacs to the mud-spattered beaters and choosing the Cadillac side. Wishful thinking it might have been, but what is America good for if not to dream the impossible dream? Certainly Dïm had come to America with that in mind, they knew that.

So they wandered into the driveway of the billionaire businessman, where the gate happened to be open because someone was leaving. They walked slowly, tentatively, hand-in-hand.

They walked in quite a ways before they saw anyone, but what they saw on the way in was amazing. America must truly be the land of opportunity. Such sumptuousness! Finally they came to the remains of the picnic food, which still looked a feast to them. For some reason they were both ravenous—it seemed like days ago that they ate their little lunch at Hank's—and they tucked in, filling plates with classic American summer food. They found a couple of chairs off to the side of some rhododendron bushes and sat down to eat in the shade. They were feeling pretty well recovered when they noticed several people staring at them with frank curiosity. There were no other brown-skinned people there except one waiter and some of the groundskeepers. Boris of course was European but Halana stood out like that one person who actually comes to a pajama party in pajamas when everyone else knows it's a joke. At least she no longer wore the headscarf, she thought, thankful that she was a modern Pakistani woman. They began to doubt that Dïm was anywhere here at this affair.

Nancy Kipp was also sitting in the shade of those rhododendrons, happy to be ignored by the remaining picnickers, and getting quite impatient to leave. Right away she noticed Boris and Halana, and her interest was piqued. Clearly these were not your typical Republican voters.

Pete and the billionaire businessman were by this time finished with their three-hole golf game and had moved on to well-aged double malt Scotch on the rocks in a little pavilion by the lake. They were having a great discussion about tax relief for the wealthy when the billionaire businessman's personal assistant came up and discreetly whispered something in his boss's ear and pointed toward the eating area.

"Well just escort them out or something," he said with a wave of his hand. "I don't know—you can take care of it however you see fit. Don't bother me with details like that."

So the assistant, who had the physique of a bodyguard more than an executive manager, hopped on a golf cart and buzzed over toward that clump of rhodies. He approached Boris and Halana with polite but firm resolve. "I'm sorry sir, but I am going to have to ask you to leave. This is a private event by invitation only." With a sweep of his arm he indicated the direction he wished them to take.

They looked at each other. Boris said, "We are looking for our son. If he is here, we wish to see him." The bodyguard replied without hesitation. Boris' accent had put him in a more authoritative mode. "He is not here. And I must insist that you leave now." He took hold of Boris' elbow and attempted to walk him away. Boris, however, was having none of it. He had seen military moves and thuggish political skullduggery all his life. All this guy had was a walkie-talkie. Boris was not afraid of him. He yanked his arm away and stared daggers at the man. By this time they had attracted a small group of onlookers.

Nancy suddenly felt moved to intervene. Her natural empathy for people would not let her sit idly by and watch while someone was mistreated. She strolled over to the trio and said pleasantly, "I'm sure it would be fine if we took these people for a little tour around the property just to see if their son is here. No one would mind, would they?" She was operating under the mistaken assumption that the son they were looking for was one of the staff.

The bodyguard, recognizing Nancy as the wife of the presidential candidate, was instantly deferential, but curt. "Of course. I'll get the cart."

Thus the four of them (Nancy decided she should accompany them just in case the guard got surly again, and besides she was bored out of her mind) got in the cart and started putt-putting around to all the various areas of the rambling estate. "Ooh—stop a minute, would you please?" she said when she spotted a waiter with a tray of champagne, and she jumped out and grabbed three glasses, handing one each to Boris and Halana, who felt that perhaps they could use a reward for a hard day, and accepted them with graceful and grateful nods of the head. The guard rolled his eyes. When they drove past where Pete was sitting with the host, Nancy waved gaily.

The billionaire businessman (a smart man) understood that these were the people he had told his assistant to get rid of. So what were they doing now riding around his estate in a cart and drinking champagne with the potential First Lady of the United States???

Hank Tells Leni about the House

Hank got out of the truck and nonchalantly walked over to Leni.

"Hi babe," he smiled. "You must have had one good day, huh? All those art people buying all your Dead stuff?" Instantly he regretted not having said the full name of the band. Of course she would know what he meant, but still.

Leni just narrowed her eyes and looked at him quizzically. "What's wrong?"

Hank stepped close to her and took her in his arms. "I'm so sorry," he murmured into her hair.

Leni's whole body turned to ice and she sagged in his arms. "What is it? Is it Maryka? Something terrible has happened to her!" This had been her worst fear ever since giving birth to her baby 25 years ago, as it is for mothers everywhere.

"No no—she's fine," Hank assured her. "Everybody's okay. Well, except your house. I guess that shower thing you were worried about was pretty bad after all. I'm so sorry I didn't take a good look at it before."

"God dammit Hank—just tell me what happened!"

So Hank proceeded to relate the sad sequence of events (minus the intimate details of the shower scene) that had resulted in major damage to her abode.

Groaning loudly, Leni walked into her shop, closed the door, continued on into the back room, and screamed at the top of her lungs. Hank had also seen this behavior before, so he wasn't too upset by it. It was her way of expressing frustration. He started gathering up sale debris and hauling everything inside. By the time Leni was finished screaming, he had everything stashed away in a somewhat organized fashion. She staggered out from the back room coughing her head off. Her lungs were not in the best shape for extended screaming. Hank took her in his arms again and stroked her hair.

"It'll be okay babe," he said, attempting to be positive. "Place probably needed a good . . ." He paused. What had it needed? A good fall down? A thorough demolishing? No, no good face could be put on this.

"Where are they now?" asked Leni.

"Who?" said Hank.

"Dïm's parents. My houseguests," she said.

"Oh," he said. "I dropped them off at the fair to see Dïm. Just now, on my way here. Maryka's at home."

"Well, I guess that's where I'm headed too. Might as well get it over with. I'll need to call the insurance company right away."

"Right." Hank nodded. "I'll follow you."

As soon as Maryka heard Leni drive up, she ran out to meet her. They fell into each other's arms and just swayed together for a long time. But Leni's curiosity finally raised her head and she grimly started toward the A frame, holding onto Maryka for support.

Hank had arrived and sat respectfully in his van until the women started moving in the direction of the house, then he quickly got out and caught up with them. He didn't hear any popping or cracking sounds, so he hoped the collapsing had stopped. They opened the door to the daylight basement laundry room. Leni gasped and let out a shaky moan. She looked up through the gaping hole that had been the bathroom floor. The external wall still hung there, the trompe l'oeil revealing a scene from paradise. Memories of making those tiles, the early days of the shop, Maryka as a baby, her mother Mary Kay watching the work progress and cheering her on—all these swirled around in Leni's heart and mind. Hank was the only other person who had been around then that also remembered all those things, and suddenly Leni threw herself into Hank's arms and began sobbing her heart out. He held her tenderly and stroked her back.

"Can I go in there?" Leni asked Hank plaintively.

"Not until I check it out. No way you want the rest of that floor collapsing on you," he replied firmly. "I guess I should do that now." He grabbed a stepladder from where it rested against the back wall of the laundry room, situated it under the jagged edge of floor, and cautiously climbed two steps up, bringing his head close enough to inspect at close range the joists remaining. It appeared the water had stopped pretty cleanly at that joist just beyond the toilet, and Hank could see no signs of rot there at all. He very gingerly tried to jiggle it with one hand and when it did not move, he jiggled it a little harder. Nothing. He breathed a big sigh of relief.

"Okay," he said, climbing down. "The rest of the upstairs should be safe. And the downstairs too. It's not going to collapse any further."

"Well what should we do now?" asked Maryka. She was still feeling a little queasy and really wanted to just have a lie-down on her bed and not think about anything.

"I want to be left alone for a little," said Leni. "But I suppose we have to figure out what to do about the houseguests." She shot a slightly baleful look at Hank.

"What?" said Hank. "You're blaming me for this? Because I put them in the guest room here? It is a plain fact that this is the only house that has room for guests, even still. We'll have to clear out another room for them to sleep in. Of course there is the issue of water, since I shut it off outside. But we can get around that for now by bringing in water to use for cooking and drinking. No bathing here for a while." He was feeling a little snappish at being blamed for this.

Leni knew he was right, as always. She heaved one last sigh and went down the hall toward the room where she had stored all of her mother's things.

* *

Low-Speed Chase

As Nancy and the Petrovskys rode around the estate looking for Dïm, it gradually became clear to Nancy that he was not a staff person. Halana distinctly recalled Hank saying that he was at some kind of fair. This was not a fair. This was a picnic. Nancy came to the fuzzy understanding through her champagne haze that he must be across the street at the place she had seen from the helicopter. Also she had gleaned from Boris and Halana's attempts at communicating, that they had had a very long strange trip, and the Grateful Dead song of that name came unbidden to mind, possibly triggered by her unconscious memory of seeing Leni's poster this morning on the way through town. That brought up images of colorful, tie-dyed clothes, memories of the Bay Area in the late '60s, and twinges of regret for things not done. Suddenly Nancy had a great idea—she would take Boris and Halana across the road to the fair to find their son! She would just tell the bodyguard to drive the golf cart over there. No problem.

Which is what she did. The assistant/bodyguard's mouth sewed itself into a tight line when she asked him to drive them across the road, but he realized he had no choice. Her husband was the presidential candidate.

Meanwhile the billionaire businessman had decided the situation needed his attention after all, so he flagged down another golf cart and jumped in to follow the one Nancy and the Petrovskys were in. Pete wasn't sure what he was supposed to do. He stood up when his host did, who beckoned him to come along. They took off in the direction that Nancy and the bodyguard had been going. The two carts weren't so very far apart but these were the kind of golf carts that can only go about 12 mph, so the distance between them remained constant.

There were still people taking helicopter rides, and from 300 feet up, as they were preparing to land, those people looking down saw what looked like a high-speed chase in slow motion involving two golf carts heading toward the entrance to the estate or, in this case, the exit. People being the curious gawkers that they are, when those folks got out of the copter they jumped into golf carts to follow the action. Emerald Valley Ranch owned three golf carts for staff use but had rented four more for the big occasion today. The four people who got off the copter ride took one and headed for the gate. That still left four for other guests to use, so they figured it would be fine.

* *

Hank

Hank was pacing. He felt he should be doing something to help someone. Leni wanted to be alone in her house, and Maryka didn't feel too well. He wondered how it was going with Dïm and his parents, and decided he should run up to the equestrian park where the fair was being held and check on them. Dïm could be pretty useless sometimes—they might need a real adult. So he wrote a quick note to Leni and Maryka telling them where he was going, jumped in his truck, and took off.

Just as he was nearing the entrance to the equestrian park, he had to come to a full stop because there was a golf cart crossing the road from the entrance to Emerald Valley Ranch and headed toward the WAAOW fair. Well what the?? There was one car in front of him but he still had pretty good visibility, and it looked for all the world like Boris and Halana riding in that cart with a woman in polyester slacks and a red, white, and blue scarf. And they were drinking champagne!

* *

The Tune of the Fair's Venue

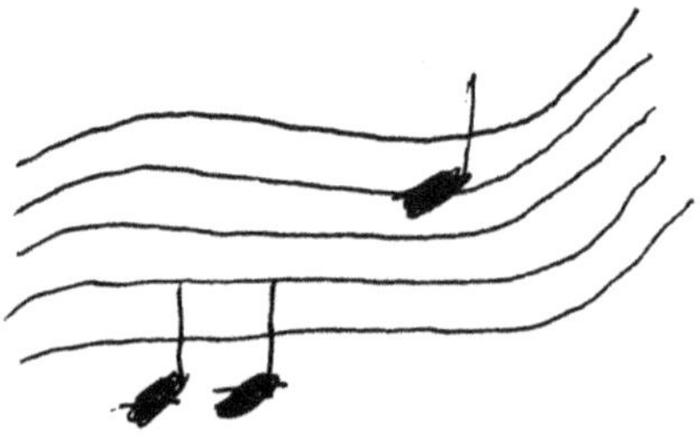

The billionaire businessman and Pete had to wait until two cars went by before they could cross the road in pursuit of the first golf cart. As they entered the park Pete happened to notice the mailbox with the number on it. 11900. Wow—CC and then the D of the octave above the first C, and then two rests. That really shot you way up there and left you hanging in the air didn't it? Anything might happen there.

* *

Leni and Mary Kay

Leni went into the spare room downstairs across the hall from the ill-fated laundry room, the room where she had stored all of her mother's things. She needed to commune with Mary Kay. She did this sometimes and always felt better for it. Mary Kay was even there for her from beyond the grave. Except there was no grave. Well, technically there was, at least a spot where her ashes were supposed to join those of her husband, Leni's dad. Only Leni had not been able to let go of her ashes. She secretly had brought them home and stashed them on the shelf of the closet of that room. And sometimes when she felt overwhelmed by life, she would come down here and pour out her heart to the urn (at least Mary Kay was in a nice urn and not a coffee can or something). And it seemed to Leni that someone was listening. Listening in a loving way, and somehow responding, though not in words but feelings, images. Presenting the longer perspective. Being grateful for life's many blessings. Restoring her soul, as it were. Leni was not sure she believed in a soul, but she could not deny this thing that happened when she went downstairs to the urn. Also sometimes it gave her the tingly head.

So that's where she went now. She had to get the stepladder from the laundry room to reach the shelf where the urn rested, blissfully unaware of the collapsing house around it. Or was it? She? Did you see and know everything beyond the grave? Well, that was certainly one of life's hotly contested questions over the millennia, wasn't it? It was a nice urn. The softest pink, Calais Soft Pink Brass. Not the priciest one by any means (in fact one of the very least expensive) but it was classy, perfect for a lady from the south such as Mary Kay. Vaguely the shape of a cookie jar, but many urns were.

Leni was named Lenore after several maternal ancestors in her line, the first being Mary Kay's great grandmother, born in 1845 and named Lenore for the recent and popular Edgar Allan Poe poem of that name, which celebrates the life of a young woman deceased too soon and rejoices in her ascension to heaven. This was always explained to the girl who received the name in the family, passed down through the decades. Leni had in the past been cheered by this and usually felt it was a fortunate name to have. Today though, she wasn't sure. Today felt like a close call. Well, not that she herself had been in danger, but it could have been her. It was her shower, wasn't it? And okay, she wasn't young anymore but she wasn't past her *prime*. It wasn't too late for her. Wait—too late for what, she asked herself. To have a life? What did that even mean? She had a life. To have everything she wanted? Life is not something you get just the way you want it and then it stays that way, Leni was wise enough to know that. Things keep on happening. Sometimes things that happen are great and fine and wonderful and other times they are a pain in the ass, scary, dark, or sad. It was Leni's habit to get the urn down and commune with Mary Kay to sort out the things that happened in her world. And Mary Kay would comfort her in that wordless way.

This time, Leni felt nothing in response to her admittedly self-pitying and woe-is-me barrage of bathroom collapse. Oh God. What was her mom saying to her? By not saying anything. Oh God. Time to grow up, figure it out.

What Leni had not wanted to hear. Perhaps Mary Kay was tired of residing on the shelf. Perhaps she wanted to be properly laid to rest, or scattered. Hmm . . . yes maybe this near disaster would be the catalyst Leni needed to . . . to . . . what? Stop leaning on her mom like she had her whole life? Using her mom as an emotional crutch?

Leni was seized with a moment of initiative. She grabbed up that urn containing what was left of Mary Kay and darted outside with it in her arms. No time like the present. She went to get Hank but then noticed his note to her that he had gone up to the WAAOW fair to check on the Petrovskys. All right. So be it. She would go up there too, though she had not thought she would.

She went to get Maryka to go with her and do the deed, but Maryka was acting rather wimpy and said she needed to run into town and get something first, and would meet her up at the equestrian park in a bit.

Leni looked around and pondered the vehicle situation. It was like a game of musical cars there. Let's see, Maryka had borrowed her Toyota (the Peugeot had long since given up the ghost and rested in rusty glory under a big willow on the property), and she had borrowed a Subaru from Hank. She supposed she should stick with that arrangement. She went back inside and upstairs to her bedroom to get a sweater in case they were out after dark. Even in the summer it cooled off of an evening when the sun went down. In the hallway she stopped at the door to the bathroom, took a deep breath, and peered in. Dear Lord. It must have been terrifying to be in that tub when it tore loose. Those poor people. Still, she mused, what had they been doing so energetically?

* *

Nancy at the WAAOW Fair

Nancy Kipp felt exhilarated. Look at her, going way out of bounds like this. Coloring outside the lines, as it were. She had no idea what would happen next, and that was such an unknown feeling for her. In public life, everything is pretty much scheduled, scripted, and stultifying.

As they drove up the winding driveway to where the fair was, she could see the slope where gleeful but tired children on that giddy hysterical edge were still slipping and sliding down the water-slick plastic and landing in the mud. She did not see any supervisory adults there. Her heart leapt in her breast. There was one lackadaisical teenager in charge of the hose, keeping the Slip 'n Slide wet and occasionally rinsing the mud off the urchins, but he did not appear to have any ambitions of authority. They continued to where the main area of the booths started, and there they had to leave the cart and walk in. Nancy had no idea what they were looking for but assumed that Boris and Halana would recognize their son when they saw him.

Goodness—she had never seen so much armpit hair on women. She remembered one of her professors in college who used to have students over to his apartment on Friday nights to talk about philosophy. A salon, he called it. She had gone once. He was married to some kind of foreigner, Italian maybe, who had long thick dark hair, a thatch of which was under her arms.

Nancy had been shocked at that but in the intervening years had forgotten about it, as she did not run in circles of non-shaving women. Seeing that it was apparently in vogue here, she wondered if she could get used to that for herself. She didn't think so.

She stared open-mouthed at everything she saw. Therapeutic Laughing? My, she really hadn't kept up, had she? "The Natural Philosopher—wonder what that's about?" she mused, and went closer; Boris and Halana had drifted off in their own direction, which was fine, wasn't it?

Nancy did not understand much of what she saw on the posters of the Natural Philosopher, but she thought Pete would appreciate it—it seemed to be something about the mathematics of music. She did like the tie-dyed clothing though.

As if on cue, here came Pete with his compadre, the billionaire businessman. They were trying to appear cool, but Nancy could tell Pete was gaping a little internally. None of them were accustomed to being in the minority anywhere, and here they were clearly in the minority. In fact the two well-dressed men strolling with their drinks in hand, obviously not fruit smoothies but Scotch on the rocks, were even getting some curious stares from the other WAAOW fairgoers. They spied Nancy and sped up to catch her before she got away.

"Nance—wait up!" called Pete, though she was already standing still doing just that.

"What's going on? Why did you take the golf cart and come over here? And who are those people you had in the cart with you? And where are they now?"

Pete always was one to get straight to the point. But just as she was about to explain everything, at least to the best of her knowledge, he caught sight of the posters she had been looking at. He was hooked instantly. His brain perked up through the fog of champagne and Scotch, his eyebrows furrowed with interest, and he stepped forward to engage further with the Natural Philosopher himself. Nancy knew then she had time to explore some more, and signaled to him that she was moving in another direction. He nodded and waved her away. "I'll find you in a minute," he said. "I just want to check this stuff out."

* *

Maryka

Maryka was at the pharmacy, staring at the home pregnancy tests in the feminine hygiene aisle. She actually felt more composed than she had let on back at home but still, her heart was fluttering a bit. She had of course considered the possibility of this. The ironic symmetry of her repeating what her mother had done by becoming a single mom. Although her circumstance was entirely different, in that the father was present. Psychoanalyzing herself, which she was prone to do (that psych class in college had really sunk in), she might say that perhaps she was refusing, or ignoring, or deferring Dïm's proposal of marriage in order to increase the chances of a pregnancy out of wedlock, so her mother would feel emulated. (?) But then Maryka did not want to raise a child without a father, like she had been raised. Not that it was horrible or anything, but she just saw how hard it was, how much work her mother was always doing. And she even had the support and help of Mary Kay and Hank. No, Maryka had long ago decided that she would not be a single mom.

So she supposed that now was the time to make a decision. If it turned out positive. But late period, sore breasts, queasy and tired? Pretty solid clues. It looks like Dïm's parents may have timed their visit perfectly for a big announcement, she thought. Or perhaps they should wait. Lots of people waited until the third month, when chances of a miscarriage were lower, so as not to . . . what? Put their family through the grief of dashed hopes? Suffer that awful death alone, then—is that what we should do? Maryka mused about all these things. But at least she would agree to marry him. Yes, and that would be the big announcement. Dïm would be ecstatic. They might have to even do it while the Petrovskys were here. Or, wait . . . did they expect Dïm to come back and have a big fat Pakistani wedding? She knew he had relatives on his mother's side there, maybe a lot of them. They had never talked about this specifically.

Well in any case, she thought, life was getting interesting.

* *

Leni at the Fair

Leni was not that long behind Hank, but she had to park way down in the pasture across the street and walk back up to the park. (Hank had a friend who lived right next door to the park, so he had been able to park there and cut across the field.) And it was up—the park was named Paradise Ridge because it was atop one of the many ridges that the last glacier had carved out of the island, alternating of course with ravines. Leni's lungs were not in the best shape, seeing as how she was still a smoker after all these years; plus she was carrying the pink pearlescent cookie jar-shaped urn that held Mary Kay, who was admittedly not that heavy anymore, but still. By the time she got up to the driveway entrance, she really needed to sit down and catch her breath.

The last golf cart carrying slightly tipsy Republicans curious as to why lots of guests, including the host and the presidential candidate, had been seen heading over here, was just crossing the road when Leni arrived gasping for breath and clutching her precious cargo. The woman in the cart—the stern fiscally conservative one who had been on the first copter ride with Pete and Nancy (Bernice was her name and she was slightly less stern after a few drinks)—recognized the urn. She was an organized person and had her advance directives all figured out and in place, all arrangements made and paid, and that urn was the very same one she had picked out for herself, Calais Soft Pink Brass.

"Oh stop and let's pick up this poor tired woman and give her a lift into the park," she called out to the person driving the cart, which caused the other riders to turn and stare at her. Bernice ignored them. "Come on, dear," she waved to Leni, indicating that she should step into the cart. "You look exhausted—we'll give you a ride."

Well, Leni had never advocated accepting rides from total strangers, but if ever there was clearly a no-danger-at-all situation, this was it. She knew when to let the universe offer her a gift. She climbed in and said a sincere thank you, remembering the manners her dear southern mama had taught her.

Bernice, in turn, politely did not even glance at Leni's outfit—a tie-dyed T-shirt (in fact it was one of the Natural Philosopher's creations, an early version of a guitar-shaped mass of color in the center) and some old bell-bottom jeans that still fit her (to go along with the whole Grateful Dead theme of the sale)—but graciously said, "You're welcome," even feeling slightly embarrassed at her own elegant but severe beige linen suit accessorized with a single wide gold belt.

Bernice didn't know how to ask Leni about the urn, which she was burning to do, so there were several moments of awkward silence in the cart, during which she kept stealing glances at the urn, and then at Leni's face to see if she might be about to reveal the reason she was carrying an urn to a hippie festival. Bernice knew it was a hippie festival from some talk at the picnic she had overheard. Finally she asked, "Are you going to any particular thing at the fair?"

"No," said Leni. "I'm trying to find my daughter and my . . . (what was Hank to her? Her boyfriend?) . . . my friend Hank."

"Ah," said Bernice, though that clarified nothing.

What was her plan exactly, questioned Leni. What did she want Hank and Maryka to do? She obviously was on one of her impulsive bursts again; what had been her thoughts when she grabbed the urn and took off for the fair? She guessed she had thought they would take the ashes down to the beach and sprinkle them, with some sort of impromptu little ceremony. She knew Maryka would want to be involved, and she thought probably Hank would too. Yes, that still sounded like a good idea to her. She would find her family here and they would do this thing together.

When they got to where you had to leave the carts and walk in, she distractedly said another thank you to a disappointed Bernice and started walking and searching the crowd for two familiar faces.

Inevitably, she saw a lot of familiar faces. Living in a small town for your whole life leads to that sort of thing, knowing a lot of people. Besides she had for all those years sat and listened to her customers gossip at the ceramics store while they glazed their pieces and smoked, so she knew stuff about people too. "Oh there's that boy, what's-her-name's grandson, the one that did that thing at the school that time," Leni talked to herself as she walked. "And there's those twins, playing music—aren't they darling." She remembered when they were born. And there was Dora, the regal looking British lady in her favored outfit—a lavender long-sleeved snowsuit, high rubber boots, and of course her signature triple layered hat atop her elegant white blond French twist, toting her little white lap dog. And there was sweet little Lorene, the tile lady. Leni had admired her for years, and secretly thought that Lorene might be herself in an alternate universe. She was a true ceramic artist, not like Leni. She had made choices in her life opposite to what Leni had, and had lived with those choices through some difficult challenges, but lived life fully, on the edge. Her tiles were vibrantly colored whimsical images captioned with saucy, reverent, or lyrical sayings, unique in the pottery world. She had dedicated herself to her art though poor as dirt and a single mom of two and pulled herself up to fame and fortune. Leni felt awestruck and tongue-tied around her. She smiled at her and gave a half wave, and Lorene returned the smile full force with all of her nearly five feet earnestly poured into that interaction, the way she always did everything. Ah well, thought Leni. The road not taken.

She saw one face that looked familiar just from today. Some of the Wildisle art people had set up a presence at the fair, one of whom had briefly stopped in at her shop this morning. Leni veered in that direction, only to find Hank there already. He was completely entranced by some abstract watercolors called "Firewood." He and the artist, a very attractive woman that Leni judged to be in her early forties, were engrossed in a conversation about it. Leni felt a slight twinge of jealousy. Hank had never appreciated art so much before, she thought.

She slowed down, so as not to seem like she was barging in on their fascinating chat, but Hank caught sight of her.

"Leni!" He appeared surprised to see her here. "Look at these paintings! Don't they just have the exact colors and textures of the madrone firewood when we cut it?" Of course he immediately included her fully in the conversation without a hint of anything else. Leni felt for the hundredth time that Hank was such a better person than she was, and effortlessly. She agreed that the paintings were quite wonderful.

Hank noticed then that she was carrying the urn with Mary Kay's ashes. He tried to wrap his brain around that but found he could not. He remembered the urn from the memorial service but had not seen it since then. He assumed it had been dealt with in the usual manner. What in God's name was Leni doing with it in her arms here and now?

* *

Boris and Halana and Dïm

The fair was small enough that ten minutes of strolling around was enough to see everything without stopping and looking at any one thing. Boris and Halana walked past the food booths quickly (they were quite full by this time), only scanning the faces to see if one belonged to their son. They walked past the children's activities and the stage where the music was. They didn't think he would be there, having never shown that much interest in music. Besides, you could hear it blasting for miles around probably, they thought. No need to stand right next to it, you would go deaf.

Finally they came to the concentration of shelters and booths that was really the meat of the fair, and there was Dïm's tent, situated so that the open door was facing away from the breeze. They almost didn't see him, because a small crowd of onlookers was watching him make his design of colored sand, but then they heard his voice. He was explaining to his audience the symbolism of the colors he was choosing, and the intention and meaning of his creation, which was world unity (the theme of the fair). His parents looked at each other with a familiar wry smile. They recognized his bullshit.

Dïm paused to glance up at his admirers, to see if they were sympathetic to his efforts, and drew in a surprised gasp.

“Ammi! Abba!” he cried, dropping his tool and messing up the part he had just painstakingly drawn. He jumped up and ran over to them and embraced them joyfully. They proceeded to engage in a long animated exchange in Urdu, which the small crowd watched with as much interest as they had the sand painting.

* *

Maryka

Maryka was still in a daze pondering her new possibilities as she walked up the drive into the fair. When she came to the part where the Slip 'n Slide was set up, she paused to peer down at the scene. She was always interested in children's activity areas. She squinted into the bright sun and frowned slightly. By now, the ground below the plastic slide was totally saturated and was a virtual pool of mud. No adult had been present to perhaps move the slide over five or ten feet, and so the same little patch of ground had been steadily taking water for hours now, combined with the constant thud of young bodies into it and feet scrambling for a foothold. It looked to Maryka like an accident waiting to happen. Many of the kids were older elementary age, but some of the youngest ones were Maryka's students at the preschool. They spied her up there looking down at them and their faces lit up with glee.

"Maryka!" they squealed, as they ran up the incline and hurled themselves at her.

"Hi!" she laughed back at them, kneeling down so as to be at their level. "What's going on?"

"We're sliding down the water slide!" they chorused spontaneously.

"How deep is the mud at the bottom?" she asked with an I'm-just-checking-for-your-safety tone of voice. "Show me how far it comes up to on your legs."

A little curly-mopped girl breathlessly and proudly announced, "It comes all the way up to here on me!" as she pointed to her waist.

"O kaaaaayyyy," said Maryka. She turned to the boy wielding the hose. "Who's in charge here?" she asked politely but authoritatively.

"Umm . . . I guess I am," he said somewhat surprised at that information.

"Well, turn off that hose. We're closing for a while. The slide needs to be moved over at least ten feet—the mud is too deep at the bottom. Haven't you been paying attention? There is such a thing as paying attention to the safety of children." This last was said with more anger than she intended. Whew. Maryka hadn't meant to go off like that, but she found the words spurting out of her mouth.

The kid looked at her quizzically. "Are you in charge now?" he asked with just the barest hint of attitude. It was hard to tell exactly how old she was. He stared pointedly at her muddy bedraggled appearance, courtesy of the urchins flinging themselves upon her. She looked down at herself. She was almost as muddy as the children.

"Yes. Yes I am, because somebody has to be responsible," she said with as much dignity as she could muster. "And hey—before you turn the hose off, spray this mud off of me, would you?" She laughed. It was so hot, the water would feel great.

The boy smiled at the kids, who were all gathered at the top watching by this time, waiting for the hose to be turned on the slide. They didn't want the slide to close, even for a little while. It wasn't exactly a conspiratorial smile and it wasn't exactly a lewd smile, but if pressed to analyze it, one might consider those words. He turned the hose full on and aimed it at her thighs and torso, even though most of the mud was at knee level.

The cold force of it knocked Maryka backwards a step or two, and she gasped with shock. And then she got into it. It really did feel good. She twirled around to get the back side as well, and then held up her hand to say stop. He stopped immediately. The children were all shrieking and laughing and begging to be sprayed themselves, which he did, obligingly. Pretty soon they were all laughing and having a good old time with no hard feelings at all. It was that kind of day.

When everyone was mud-free and soaking wet, Maryka signaled the boy to turn off the hose. She went over to him and explained, as if he were an adult, about how if they meant to keep it going, the slide would have to be moved over to drier ground. He nodded but reckoned that was more work than he wanted to do, so he just set the hose down and ambled off. A disappointed cry went up from the dripping, sunburned little people.

"It's okay—we'll just go and find some of your parents to do it. You probably should check in with them anyway." Maryka noticed how easily she slipped into the role of parent as she held their small hands and they all walked together into the fair. Maybe this would all work out after all. She could get married and have a baby. Of course Dïm would have to get a real job—that might take a spot of negotiating, but he was certainly smart enough to do something more than he was doing now.

* *

Maryka, Dïm, Boris and Halana

Maryka and her soggy brood threaded their way through the crowd, which by this time had grown to a robust 600 or so. She had told the children to find their parents and tell them they needed to help move the Slip 'n Slide, so as they spotted them, kids peeled off from the group. Two siblings still had not found their people when Maryka arrived at Dïm's tent, and the three of them trudged in as a unit.

Dïm glanced toward the movement at the entrance and his face brightened as it always did whenever he saw her. But just as quickly that look became one of surprise and embarrassed disapproval. Maryka's jersey knit sundress, normally a loose, swirling affair, was clinging to her wet body, leaving not much to the imagination. Dïm, even though he had come to America and done the college scene, still deep inside preferred the modesty in women that he had grown up with in Pakistan. And his mother was standing right there to see it too!

Halana's actual thought when she saw Maryka was that it was instant karmic justice that she should see Maryka practically naked when Maryka had seen her naked a little while before. So she was oddly not bothered by it that much; besides, she was a modern Pakistani woman.

Dïm started to introduce Maryka to his parents. In answering his questions and telling their story, they had not gotten to the part about the bathroom disaster, so Dïm had no idea they had met already, and in such a humiliating way for his parents.

“Ammi, Abba, this is Maryk—“

“Yes, we met earlier, at the house,” Halana said coolly, looking at Maryka’s nipples embossed on the soft white fabric of her dress.

“You were already at the house?” he asked.

The three of them nodded ruefully, they couldn’t help it. Dïm felt left out. Obviously there was something he was not privy to. He decided to switch the subject to something more immediate.

“Maryka—why are you soaking wet?” he demanded. He was completely unaware of the whole Slip ’n Slide activity, being inside the fair before it was set up. And too, he rarely paid much attention to children in general. He had barely noticed the ones Maryka had in tow, but now he looked at them. “And why are they wet?”

But at that exact moment, the kids in question were taken into protective custody by their parents, who happened to be in the small throng of onlookers in the tent. They were young hippie types—the dad had dreadlocks—who were not overly concerned with a little water. It was a hot day—they would dry out. They knew Maryka from the preschool, and she quickly filled them in on the situation. They smiled and nodded and made their way out of the tent with the young ones in arms, who had immediately upon seeing their parents collapsed into whining sniveling puddles and had to be carried. Maryka smiled inwardly—she saw this behavior quite often. Kids, she thought, if they had a loving supportive family, felt safe enough to be able to collapse like that when they had been overstimulated. If they were not safe in their family, that sort of thing never happened, or it happened at their peril. She tried to remember if she had been a child who had meltdowns like that. Somehow she didn't think she had. Just out of consideration for Leni, because there was only one of her.

"Well are you going to tell me or not?" Dïm was being uncharacteristically insistent about how she got wet, was Maryka's thought. She wondered if he had been a child prone to meltdowns, and whether he still sort of was.

"It was the water slide they had set up. It needed seeing to," was all the explanation she felt like giving him at that moment, and she turned back to his parents.

"Did you see Dïm's sand mandala?" she asked brightly.

* *

Leni and Hank

Hank gave a last wistful look at the watercolors of firewood as he stepped away with Leni.

"So what did the insurance company say?" After the events of the day, he wasn't sure he had it in him to ask about the urn. Best to stick to concrete matters that he could understand.

"Well of course it's Saturday so they didn't say anything. They said they would have someone return my call first thing Monday morning."

"Well it could be worse," Hank began.

Leni's eyes flared wide. "Why do you ALWAYS have to say that when bad things happen?" she demanded.

This gave Hank pause. Why indeed did he do this? It was such an ingrained habit he had never thought about it before. It was something he had heard his parents say his whole life. Descended from Scandinavian immigrants three generations back, the philosophy of "Could be worse" was deeply embedded in his family. It was a way of counting your blessings (indirectly) while simultaneously discounting one's own importance. It worked for Hank on a practical basis. He could easily imagine the ways it could actually be worse.

But he guessed some folks needed more coddling than that. They needed commiseration. Leni in particular was always seeking commiseration about something or other, he realized.

"I don't know," he said thoughtfully. "Just something I always heard said, and it seems true to me. It COULD be worse. For instance, in your case, the whole entire floor could have collapsed, and not just part of the bathroom floor. Or somebody could have been standing down at the washer putting in a load of clothes. They would have been killed. I can think of lots of ways it could be worse."

There it was. Hank in a nutshell. Leni could always count on him to give an earnest, considered, and true answer, and not rise to anger when she challenged with what could easily have been a catalyst to an argument. He was a maddeningly good man. Why did she resist him so? Why not just go with a good thing when it was right there in front of her?

"Oh Hank," was all she said. There was such an air of sadness and resignation in the way she spoke that Hank became somewhat alarmed, and decided to change the subject and ask about the urn after all. But first he sidled closer to her and draped one arm around her shoulders, giving her a little sideways hug.

"What kind of passenger you got there?" he asked, nodding his head toward the urn, though he knew very well who it was.

"You know it's Mary Kay and don't pretend you don't," she shot back. "I need you to help me . . . no," she sighed. "I WANT you to help me scatter her ashes down at the beach."

"Right now? Today? With everything else that's going on? Why?"

"I can't explain. I just have to."

"Hmm. Well if you have to, I guess." Hank knew Leni better than anyone, probably even Maryka. He knew that she was a person who acted upon impulse most of the time and did not retreat from those actions or decisions. One big example was Maryka herself. Leni had for whatever reason decided not to share her pregnancy with the father, and never looked back. Hank had been bold enough to ask her about it once or twice, and Leni had simply shaken her head, spread her hands, and said, "It's over and done. It is what it is." Which didn't really answer the questions Hank had—who was he, was Leni in love with him, how did they meet, etc etc. Because Hank was in love with her and he kind of wanted to know who his competition had been. But Leni only looked forward, never back. There are people who operate like this, and she was one.

Hank recognized the language signaling that something was one of these impulses that would be carried out, namely the words she had just spoken—"I can't explain. I just have to." Grabbing the urn was clearly an impulse she had to obey.

"So I need to find Maryka to help me too. She would want to."

"Okay." They continued then making their way through the crowd, silently, each preoccupied with private thoughts, but kind of commiserating non-verbally, Hank hoped.

* *

Nancy and Leni and Hank and Boris and Halana and Dïm and Maryka and finally Pete

Nancy Kipp sniffed her way through the crowd while Pete discoursed with Tod, the Natural Philosopher, about the vibrational planes of sounds. There may have been a funky skunky whiff of marijuana on a tuft of a breeze that led Nancy down across the broadening hillside, or maybe she was just drawn to the henna art tattoo booth. In any case, she was about to decide to get one on her hand (a tattoo) when her attention was caught by the loud hailing of someone by someone else. When she looked in the direction of the first someone, it turned out to be the Pakistani couple she had brought over in the golf cart. And she, being so fizzy and all, wanted to chime in as well.

"Hello! . . . did you find your son then?"

Boris and Halana glanced around, in their way of wordless communication, verifying that they were in fact being addressed by two separate individuals, although still somewhat far off.

Which was why Hank, addled by the day, had overshot the mark on volume and fairly bellowed out in his sweet Texas drawl, "Oh hey there! Here we are then."

"There they are," he whispered to Leni.

"Yes we did find him, thank you. He is right here." Halana smiled at Nancy, who was approaching more quickly than Hank and Leni.

"And there you are." Halana acknowledged Hank with a bow of her head as he propelled a suddenly reticent Leni along in front of him.

Nancy was hoping that Halana would introduce her to their son, who looked very exotic and handsome, but he seemed at the moment to be having a private and not altogether pleasant conversation with a young woman in a wet dress that was glued to her body.

As consolation, Nancy turned her eager curiosity onto the loose-limbed bearded man and his lady, a bleary-eyed woman with wild wiry hair who was clutching what looked like a cookie jar.

"Hello!" she said politely. "Are you friends of theirs? I helped bring them to the right party to find their son. We were across the street at a different affair."

Hank and Leni looked at each other, one bewildered and one accusatory.

"You . . . they were at the Republican picnic?" they said practically simultaneously, as much to each other as to Nancy.

"Yes, I was. You see my husband is running for President, and so we came to the picnic. It's a fundraiser for the campaign. But if you ask me, it has gone on long enough (I was getting bored)," this last whispered conspiratorially. "And I knew there was something interesting going on over here, so when these nice people showed up in the wrong place—well I don't mean *wrong* in the moral sense of course, just that it wasn't the place their son was at—I . . . saw an opportunity, and . . . oh look—here he comes now. My husband. He followed me here," this with a little chuckle. "He might be . . . I don't know if he'll . . . Oh—it looks like he changed his shirt; he must have bought a T-shirt from that guy he was talking to. Something about math—I don't understand it at all but Pete has always been a little . . ."

"Hi sweetheart!" Nancy smiled lavishly at Pete. "Isn't this fun?"

Pete had shed his oxford cloth rolled-up sleeve casual executive look and was wearing a tie-dyed T-shirt in exquisitely detailed color work in a pattern that was the visual representation of the D minor chord made famous by the Grateful Dead song "Long Strange Trip." He had in tow the billionaire businessman picnic host and the Natural Philosopher, whom Pete had taken a real shine to, insisting that he come and meet his wife. He had bought a T-shirt for Nancy too, and presented it proudly to her now.

"Oh," she said. She didn't much care for T-shirts and never wore them if she could help it now that she'd gotten plumpish—she looked like a stuffed sausage. "Thank you darling—what beautiful rich colors!" She looked at the Natural Philosopher. "You're quite talented at what you do. I admire that. I wonder though," and here she paused for a second, "would you have any other styles by chance? Could I look around and choose something a little more, well loose and maybe a bit swirly?" Oh, she was really stepping out of herself today.

"Of course you may," Tod graciously enthused. "In fact I do happen to have the cutest jacket in a style that may be just what you had in mind. You may want to change the buttons is all," he said, as if she were a co-designer. He had the most appealing southern accent, the kind Nancy really liked. "Shall we go look right now? No time like the present—hah! Since it's a present—get it?" He started to take Nancy's elbow and guide her back to his booth.

Pete looked askance at Tod. How could he be . . . be . . . like that when he had the mind of a mathematical and mystical genius? He wanted Tod to explain to Nancy the things on the posters, so that she could join him in these metaphysical musings that he loved in his spare time. Now this was turning into a shopping spree for her instead. And . . . was there a hint of a flirtation? But no, Pete had had enough alcohol to reach the point of paranoid delusions once in his life, and this was not it. This is what separates people of character from the rest—the ability to tell when they are not making wise choices and to change direction. So he just let that go, a tiny leaf blowing across the screen of his mind and then gone, as Bob Ross might have said. Pete had done some Zen reading in his life. He was evolved.

Meanwhile Halana, staring at Maryka's nipples, had become aware of a sensation underlying everything else she was experiencing: her pelvic floor still throbbed with unfulfilled desire. Her hand crept toward Boris' hand and snuck into its familiar shelter. He had also been noticing Maryka's wet exposure, and he instantly understood Halana's unspoken wish. Their heads nodded together and a few soft words were murmured, and then they turned and with polite smiles and gestures, made their way out of the tent, indicating they would return.

* *

The Earth Moved

The equestrian park at which the WAAOW fair was being held was a sprawling 43 acres of former military missile launch site. When the federal government decided the facility was no longer needed, a park commission had sprung up on the island to receive the land and do something else with it. It was used primarily by the local 4-H group and the Pony Club for their members to hold horse events of all kinds. They were always busy improving the site, raising funds for this or that, and making trails for riding through the verdant acres of forested hills. However, there were still huge areas of concrete slabs and small cinder block military-style small buildings like a guardhouse.

Today it seemed every square foot of the site was occupied. Campers had set up tents everywhere, even atop the sand arena for the horse shows, and of course all the displays, music stages and food booths, and swarms of fairgoers tromping around amongst it all made for a lack of private space.

But Boris and Halana were experienced at secret trysts in a crowded place, so they were not deterred. Holding hands, they traipsed nonchalantly in the general direction of the trees. And there they found a trail leading downhill into the woods—a wide, grassy path for the horses to ride on, and even run and jump on. Jumps had been built, jumps of all different styles and shapes, just like at a real horse jumping competition, only rustic and made out of logs or split rails.

They came upon one that was a triangular-shaped pile of poles, about ten feet long and maybe three feet high, but wide at the bottom and rising to a single log at the top. It was in the shade. Oddly, there were no people down here at all. No campers, no booths, not even any kids exploring. Presumably they were all at the Slip 'n Slide, thought Halana, who was rapidly assessing the situation for her tryst criteria, mainly privacy and comfort. The jump looked like it held possibilities for a certain amount of comfort—some slope you could lean back on while supported underneath by the ground. She wondered if it would all fall down if you put any pressure on it—like a toy log thing. Did they have ways of holding it together? But no—the logs would have to be loose so that if the horse nicked it, it would fall apart—wasn't that how it worked? Hmm.

They went around to the far side of the jump. Boris looked back to see how far from the crowds they were and nodded once. He took off the lightweight jacket he had worn for three solid days and spread it on the ground. Halana reached out and gently pushed on the fourth log up. It didn't move. She sank down to the soft earth and left her knees up, in a way that drove Boris mad with desire. Halana had taken advantage of her trip to America as an opportunity to dress slightly less modestly than she did at home. Today she was wearing an open chemise made of fine, gauzy, see-through material of a rich amber color, with a burgundy camisole underneath, and cool beige linen loose-fitting pants. When she settled into her knees-up pose, she looked like some exotic floral specimen waiting to be discovered. Boris could have gazed upon her for hours. But . . . their situation precluded a long drawn-out leadup. They could faintly hear the thrumming beat of the reggae music happening above and a little to their left and through the woods. The beat was so happy and so dancy that anybody's second chakra would open right up. They smiled and she pulled him down to her waiting and willing body.

And so it came to pass that for a second time that day they were in the throes of passionate lovemaking, nearly to the brink of ecstasy (they were flat on the ground by now because the logs had seemed a little too rolly when things got rocking), when they heard, then felt a rumbling sensation. It was for Boris, the orchestration to the grand finale of his fireworks, a great tympanic accompaniment to perhaps his biggest explosion ever, the adrenalin of the whole day having built up in him with no outlet now being allowed to burst forth.

Halana, whose eyes had shot open when she felt the rumble, could intermittently see over Boris' convulsing back. What she saw was horrifyingly unreal, something you never expect to see, something outside the realm of experience entirely. The earth was rippling like waves on the water. Her hands gripped Boris hard and she screamed. He thought at first that she was screaming in pleasure, but then realized that it was definitely a terrified scream. He stopped his writhing, pushed up on his arms, and looked wildly at the land buckling all around them. Oh. My. God. First they made the bathroom collapse and now their passion had made the earth shudder. What was happening?

He did not have long to ponder this question though, because the poles of the jump had been jostled free of their formation by the bucking forest floor and were rolling down toward Halana's face, which was right below the pile. Boris did the only thing his instinct told him to do—shield her by making his own body into a shell and taking the blows himself.

* *

Leni

Leni stared after Nancy Kipp as she walked chummily away with Tod, the Natural Philosopher and tie-dye master, to go back to his booth and get a jacket instead of a T-shirt, followed by Pete trying to catch up, which of course he did easily. The billionaire businessman had gotten tired of the WAAOW fair and made his escape back to his side of the tracks, as it were.

Tod had not even acknowledged Leni, even though they had once had a torrid fling. That was years ago. Her memories of it were vivid snippets of passion, his smell, his words, his intellect. She had realized at the time of course that nothing would come of it, but still savored every sweet moment. So she felt slightly hurt when he appeared to not notice her at all standing not five feet away from him. I mean, what was that? Couldn't they be friends? Couldn't he at least say hello? Did he actually not see her?

Leni shook her head, as if to clear it. She was still trying to take in and process everything that had happened that day to which had just been added the fact that somehow Dïm's parents had been at the Republican picnic and somehow gotten friendly with the candidate for President and his wife. And then Boris and Halana had just slipped away. Where did they go and when would they return? And then the Tod thing. She turned to Hank, naturally. He had the same bewildered look on his face that she felt must be on hers.

His, however, was a little more bemused. Leni could see that he was holding back a smile, and she could tell that he was probably also getting antsy to get back home and see to all the suddenly necessary arrangements and that he was just generally done with being here at this hippie-dippie fair. She was correct in all that. She knew this man so well.

Leni cleared her throat. "So." There was a long pause. "Well, I guess now would be the time to do this thing, then, right?" she said, nodding at the urn she carried and glancing over to where Maryka and Dïm were. They did not appear to be arguing anymore. Maryka seemed to be looking at a small box and Dïm had a goofy look on his face. This gave Leni a start—instantly her alarm hackles went up. That goofy look could only mean one thing, or maybe two. Either it was an engagement ring box and she had agreed to marry him, or it was a pregnancy test box. She elbowed Hank, meaning for him to look over there. But of course it only drew his attention to the rib that she had bothered.

"What?" Hank was irked and confused. "Sure, I guess it would be the time to do that if that's what you came to do. I don't see how that rated an elbow in the ribs though."

"Oh Hank." Caught once again by the pureness and goodness of Hank, so literal and concrete and in the moment. "I'm sorry." She dropped her voice to a whisper. "I wanted you to look over there at Maryka and Dïm. What do you think they're doing?"

Hank looked to the corner of the tent, where Dïm had his arms around Maryka and they were starting to slowly walk toward the door of the tent, heads together. There was an unmistakable air about them of brand new but joyous confidence.

"I'd say they might be going to sneak off just like his folks just did," and his chuckle escaped at last.

Leni frowned at him but had to agree that it did look like that when she glanced over there too.

"Maryka—wait!" Leni called after them, but they were out of the tent now and speeding up to a brisk trot.

"Shit!" cried Leni. Now they were the only ones there, she and Hank, just standing there at the ridiculous colored sand "mandala" at the stupid WAAOW fair. "Now what?"

"Well," began Hank, "we should probably . . ." But just then a great low growl arose from the bowels of the earth, and the ground starting undulating beneath their feet. Leni gasped. Was this the Big One they always said would hit the region someday? Oh my God—it feels like it, she thought, watching in disbelief. Suddenly a swell rose up right under Leni and she plopped down on her tailbone, throwing her arms out to catch herself. The urn flew up in the air, turned a somersault, and spilled its contents all over Leni, whose upturned face watched the whole thing as if in slow motion.

She felt her mother showering down upon her, the rough chunky ashes of white char but also Mary Kay's spirit, and her love, mainly love and assurance, blessed assurance, as the song says. Gleaming silver light. Assurance that she was good enough. In fact, more than good enough. Glittering golden light. Forgiveness for everything. And gratitude. And joy. And laughter. And permission to be good to yourself. And gratitude for everything. Amen. Deo Gratias.

* *

Hank

Hank managed to keep his footing when the swell that threw Leni into the air passed under his feet.

"Well if that doesn't take the cake," was his first thought. "An earthquake AND a partially collapsed house on the same day." This was followed closely by the panicky realization that those two things were not a good combination, and by an urgent desire to get home quickly and see if the earthquake had caused more collapse.

Then another swell came so quickly that he lurched and lost his balance, ending up on the ground next to Leni. "Hmm," he thought in that calm place that he always had in part of his mind, "could this be the Big One they are always predicting? It seems to be going on and on."

He watched as the urn full of Mary Kay's ashes did a slow flip in the air and rained down upon Leni.

"Oh great—that's just all she needs right now. This might be Leni's worst day ever." He imagined having to crawl all over the ground trying to recapture Mary Kay's remains once the shaking stopped. And then an amazing thing happened. He looked on in disbelief as Leni's face changed from horror and fear to serenity and joy. She was covered with white powdery stuff and beaming, and yes, even laughing. That's when she did the most extraordinary thing of all—she rolled toward Hank and started kissing his face all over until they were both white-faced. As the shaking subsided and it began to seem like it was over, they lay in each other's arms, exhausted but smiling—Leni with new hope and a great sense of peace, Hank with relief that Leni was not distraught, and complete acceptance of her affection without a clue as to why it happened.

* *

Maryka

The young couple escaping from the tent where all their parents were giggled as they ran toward the porta-potties. There were no large ones empty so they squeezed into a regular one. Maryka took the tube out of its box. It looked pretty straightforward—the little window where lines would appear—plus for positive and minus for negative. Makes sense, she thought. There were illustrated examples next to the window just for clarity. She took the cap off the tube and gazed at the flat strip of fiber sticking out about an inch.

"Well here goes nothing," she said to Dïm, and sat down almost on the toilet seat but with room to stick her hand holding the tube under her stream. She waited for the urine to come but it would not. It was too awkward in the crowded porta-potty and with Dïm standing right there, and with trying to position the tube so it would catch enough of the stream to work.

"Hmm—I guess I'm going to need a little privacy. Could you wait outside?"

Dïm was happy to oblige, being slightly uncomfortable himself in that intimate situation.

Finally she was able to accomplish the tricky operation. Now she had the tube in one hand and the other hand was holding up her wet dress, and she needed toilet paper to wipe herself. The pregnancy test instructions said it would take a minute before the results appeared. Maryka looked around for somewhere to put it that wouldn't be filthy, but there really wasn't any flat surface except right next to the seat, so she set it down gingerly while she wiped herself and pulled up her panties. Then she unlocked the door to let Dïm come in again so they could look at the test results together, but not before sneaking a glance at it herself. She wanted that small special moment of alone time with the idea of a baby inside her. There did indeed seem to be a plus sign emerging on the blank screen of the test tube. She felt a buzz the likes of which she had never felt. And then it became more than a buzz—it became a downright roar, at least inside the can she was in. The metal floor started vibrating underneath her feet and suddenly the left side of the can rose up slightly. Just before it dumped Maryka outside onto the ground she saw the tube slide into the open hole full of piss and shit.

* *

Dïm

Dïm was standing a little ways from the Sani-can so as not to have to inhale so much of that smell. His mind was racing with the implications of what he was about to learn. So much would change—he told himself he knew that much. But then one never really understands the extent of that change with a third person in your immediate orbit until you experience it. Would he really have to get a job? He had no idea what kind of job he could possibly get. But if it meant that Maryka would marry him and then his immigrant status would be secure, well of course there was no contest.

Suddenly the ground burped, the door of the outhouse flew open, and Maryka lurched into his arms. He wasn't expecting this and it threw him off balance, and the two of them rolled to the ground, which was still burping.

"What's happening?" he and Maryka asked simultaneously. All around them people were screaming and frantically running in all directions at once, or else just sitting down on the ground and gaping.

"Earthquake," Maryka said in a shaky voice. And then abruptly it was over, and there was a lull of quiet while everyone waited to see if it was truly over.

"Where's the pregnancy test?" Dïm asked.

Maryka gestured sadly at the outhouse and said, "In the hole."

Dïm looked at the outhouse. Imagined himself diving into that slurry of repulsive waste matter to find the test, imagined it as a metaphor for the whole baby/child effort—lots of poop, lots of throwing up no doubt, and everything involved that would be so unpleasant and messy.

"Did you see the results?" he asked.

Maryka hesitated for the barest second. "No," she fibbed slightly. For in that second she had read his mind, read his uncertainty, and his self-centered idea of what parenthood would be like. Maybe she wasn't ready for this. Maybe he wasn't ready for this.

"Well that's okay—we can get another one, right?" he said.

"Right," she agreed. They got up and shook themselves off and headed back to the tent.

* *

Nancy and Pete

Pete Kipp was deeply absorbed in trying to describe to Tod the Natural Philosopher some paintings that he had seen of mathematical equations that described certain specific arcs and parabolas. His arms swept across an imaginary canvas as he enthused about the incredible beauty of these paintings. The amazing colors—vivid gold and reds, and the subjects were Euclidean geometry, the scale of Archimedes, and so forth. Tod was following it closely, nodding with understanding and fascination, and expressing a desire to see them. Pete couldn't remember the name of the artist, was the only problem.

Meanwhile Nancy was trying on the tie-dyed jacket that Tod had shown her. It really was more her style—a short puffed-out cotton brocade jacket, gathered at the bodice, elbow-length sleeves, and a single large button at the top of the neckline. Yes, this was definitely better than a T-shirt, much more flattering.

Suddenly the ground on which they stood gave way and started bucking. Nancy screamed and frantically looked around for something to get under. She dove for the table that held Tod's assortment of non-hanging clothing.

"Pete!" she shrieked. "Under here! Get under here!"

Pete seemed almost annoyed at having been interrupted in his conversation with Tod. It was rare if not altogether unheard of for him to find someone who shared his love of cosmic mathematical philosophy, and he was loath to stop expounding. It was as if he barely noticed the ground doing anything unusual. He looked at Nancy under the table like you would look at a child who was tugging incessantly on your shirt.

"You don't need to be under something if you're outside, you stupid cow!" he said way too loudly to pretend he hadn't, although he was horrified by the way it hung there in the air for all to hear again and again in their minds. Indeed many heads turned his way, pausing in their own panic to marvel at how rude he was to his own wife.

Nancy herself was too stunned to say or do anything. Her face became a burning red ball of humiliation. She had been raised in California practicing earthquake drills her entire school career. The mantra to get underneath something had been drummed into her long-term memory for decades. Was it so stupid to fall back on this when a big one happened? Never before had Pete ever spoken to her like this. Well. The things life can surprise you with, she thought. Well well. Now what?

One of the heads that turned their way when Pete had his outburst was that of a local news reporter who had been assigned to cover the Republican picnic. He had followed Pete over to the fair, which he then decided he should also cover. Maybe it would make a good feature story, the two juxtaposed events on the island. He was vaguely following Pete and Nancy around, although it was by chance that he was near them when the earth started rolling. The reporter immediately turned on his camera and mic, overjoyed by his unbelievable good luck to catch all this footage he hadn't planned on. He hadn't really meant to film and record Pete's decidedly unkind remark, but there it was, on the record, so to speak. So then he turned the camera on Nancy, still gripping the ground under the table of tie-dyed T-shirts and practically in tears. Instantly he regretted it—it just seemed too cruel. He turned the camera back to other random fairgoers and to the last of the rolling waves of solid ground before the tumbler was over. But still, there it was.

* *

Aftermath

Dïm and Maryka slowly made their way back to the tent, looking around to see what the damage had been from the earthquake. Not much, it turned out, although it had certainly felt like a big roller as it was happening. News coverage of the event would put it at 5.1 on the Richter scale, and a few people would report things falling off the wall. But here at the WAAOW fair the old military structures were sound as could be.

Inside the tent though, there was total destruction of one thing—Dïm's sand mandala. The rippling ground had turned the whole design into a big pile of swirling colors, and the sight of that when they entered the tent, and Leni and Hank on the ground next to it, with faces covered in white chalky stuff, at first put Maryka in mind of two naughty puppies that have made a mess of something painstakingly created by their owner who had to leave the room for a minute. She burst out laughing. And the more she laughed, the more she laughed. She could not stop, and she could not get the puppy image out of her head. And then she thought about her pregnancy test falling into the porta-potty and that made her howl even harder. Of course that kind of glee is contagious, and even though Dïm was looking at her like she had suddenly gone demented, Leni and Hank started giggling along with her, and pretty soon the three of them were holding their sides guffawing and gasping for breath.

At that moment Boris and Halana returned to the tent, looking disheveled, with dirt in their hair and on their faces. This sight struck the laughers as hysterically funny, and the hilarity went to a new level. Boris and Halana looked at each other and at Leni and Hank, on the ground with white faces, and at Dïm's ruined mandala. Halana snickered, and then the dam of travel fatigue, terror, and pent-up sexual energy broke and she abandoned all decorum. She choked, chortled, cackled, and snorted. Dïm had never seen his mother act like this. He looked at his father. A little smile started playing around on his lips, and pretty soon both of them were slapping each other on the back and whooping along with everyone else.

* *

Nancy and Pete

Sam, Pete Kipp's driver, had been patiently waiting for them to come back to the Republican picnic for the longest time. Just when he was on the verge of driving over to get them, there was an earthquake! Nick, the campaign manager, had opted out of this event in favor of another fancier event that night, and had given Sam strict instructions to have them back for the next thing by no later than 5:00.

Shit, thought Sam. Now what? I've got to go over there and find them and try to catch the next ferry, whatever it is. And it's already 3:30. And who knows if anything was damaged in the earthquake. Shit.

So he hoofed it across the street and into the WAAOW fair, where things were beginning to start up again, the musicians trying out their sound equipment, and so forth. And of course everyone talking about what had just happened. Except Pete and Nancy, when he spotted them, seemingly frozen, as in a wax tableau, in the same positions they had been in when Pete had uttered the fatal words, "you stupid cow." The reporter/photographer was locked in a staredown with Pete. They both knew the consequences of video like that in this day and age. Nancy was still sitting under the table of T-shirts.

Sam knew something wasn't right about the vibe, but never mind—he had to get them out of here.

"Hey there, Senator Kipp! I thought I'd just come over and see what happened to you guys. We really should be getting back to Seattle for the next event." He glanced tentatively at Nancy under the table. What was going on here?

Pete hesitated a moment, then squared his shoulders and replied, "Sure thing, uh . . . Sam, was it? Just give us a minute to finish things up here." With a grim last look at the photographer, who returned that look with one of his own—a grim smirk, he turned to Tod.

"I would love to correspond with you about your ideas, and I will see if I can track down the name of the artist who does the paintings I was telling you about—I think it's Michael something or other. Why don't you give me your address?"

Tod was thrilled at this recognition and inclusion. The slight problem was that he was rather a drifter, with no real permanent address that lasted any length of time. "Um, I'm going to give you my brother's address. I'm kind of in between things just now, and he will always know how to find me. He lives on the island too." He whipped out a tiny notepad from the pocket of his handsome tie-dyed vest, and a pen from where he carried it behind his ear, stashed in his salt-and-pepper wavy mane, and wrote down the address and handed it to Pete. "A real pleasure to talk with you, sir. Thank you for visiting." Then he scurried over to Nancy and held out his hand to help her up, which she gratefully accepted.

"That jacket looks just perfect on you!" he enthused. "I personally am not too fond of that button, but maybe you can find a cooler one to replace it. What do you think?"

Nancy smiled at him. "Perhaps. Thank you SO much—this is just lovely." Then she turned and walked toward the driver, losing her smile. Pete strode to catch up with her.

"Sweetheart—" he began in a low voice.

She whipped her right hand up like a stop sign so fast that he did stop. They walked on in silence. Sam was extremely uncomfortable. Clearly they were having some sort of spat. And they had all that way to walk—back out of the park, across the street, and into the estate as far as where the limo was parked.

"Um, sir—I was just wondering if you and Mrs. Kipp would like to wait here for me to bring the car around?"

Pete looked at Nancy to see what she wanted to do.

"Why don't I wait here and the two of you go and get the car?" she said with a polite smile at Sam and icy eyes for Pete. "I'll mosey out toward the road and meet you."

What choice did they have? Sam and Pete joined the hordes of people who were also leaving the fair, presumably to go home and check for quake damage, slowly making their way out to the road. As they left the park, Pete looked back at the mailbox. That number. Anything could happen there, he remembered thinking to himself about that number. Well, anything sure had. He tried not to think about what might happen with that tape the reporter had, but of course then that was all he could think about. He felt sick.

Nancy looked around for a place to sit down. She felt worn out from all the day's occurrences. She wandered a little, in search of anything to sit on—she felt rather faint. Then she heard, coming from that tent, the one where those foreign people's handsome son had been, laughter. Not just regular laughter either—unrestrained, uncontrollable belly laughs, whoops, coughing, gasping, shrieking laughter. All of that at once, a choral symphony of multiple laughers. Infectious, contagious laughter. She suddenly felt a little better, like maybe there's hope. And her curiosity was piqued. She turned her steps in that direction.

Everybody Except Pete

Nancy had taken off her own red blazer to try on the tie-dyed jacket, and then walked off and forgotten it on Tod's table in all the hoopla and drama. So when she peeked into the tent, no one at first recognized her. Then Halana looked at the rest of her and saw the kind woman who had come to their rescue at the picnic across the street and brought them over here. The fact that she was wearing a hippie garment now instead of the bright red item that made her whole outfit scream "knee-jerk patriotism" (Halana was pretty savvy when it came to the nuances of worldwide politics) struck Halana as side-splittingly funny as a commentary on something or other, and she collapsed yet again in riotous laughter. Which then the others couldn't help joining in on—it was like a teenage girl's slumber party in that way.

Nancy thought at first that they were laughing at her, but then she remembered that they had already been laughing before, and then, because somehow she had made that laughter continue by just appearing, she felt included, though she longed to know the whole joke. It was a familiar feeling to her, this vague sense of being on the outside, of not quite belonging, or not knowing the drill. Something she had lived with most of her life really. She herself was grinning widely simply by being in the orbit of six grown people in the throes of gleeful merriment. She already felt much better about life. Because it didn't take too much to make Nancy happy; she was easily satisfied and almost always on an even keel, so to speak.

Finally the faces, the cheeks, the teeth of the laughers started aching with fatigue from the workout, and they slowed to a stop, though wiping eyes and smiling persisted for some time. Their endorphin-infused bodies glowed from within, and they felt so incredibly good about life, and the whole world, despite the dire things they had experienced that very day, that their hearts were emitting that vibrational information. Which Nancy's heart then took in, though she did not know that could happen. She had no idea that for the past five years the Heartmath Institute, located not 15 miles from where she and Pete lived near Santa Cruz, had been studying and verifying this phenomenon. Nevertheless, she could have been one of their experimental subjects that day, because her heart synced up with their hearts, and it was a jolly love fest all round.

It was generally agreed upon by the six that they should just go on home and hang out together, relaxing and trying to have a semi-normal visit, though what that might look like was unclear. Nancy supposed it was past time for her to have "moseyed" out to the road to meet Pete. She sighed. They were all moseying out together when they came to the main entrance of the fair, where the giant banner was strung across the driveway.

WE ARE ALL ONE WORLD

They looked at each other. They looked at all the people around them, and then back at one another. Nodded their heads with celestial understanding looks on their faces. Nancy saw the car with Pete in it just beyond the banner, waiting for her.

Just then Tod came running up, holding Nancy's red blazer.

"You forgot this!"

"Oh," Nancy replied. She didn't want that blazer anymore. "I know—why don't you do something with it—tie-dye it—and then maybe you can return it to me, or you can sell it. I don't care. Make something beautiful out of it."

Tod grinned and gave Nancy a thumbs-up, then gave her a quick little side hug and a peck on the cheek. She blushed and all of a sudden felt absurdly, ridiculously happy.

* *

Acknowledgments

I have many people to thank for being early readers. First of all, my writing group: Susan Nyman, Beth White, Antonia Greene, Pattie Hanmer, and most of all Catherine Johnson. They listened to each of my chapter by chapter installments, some of which were inspired by writing prompts we had for our group. Catherine kindly read the whole thing when I was finished and provided extensive notes, sort of a first editing.

My most enthusiastic supporter and cheerleader was Marie Bradley, who encouraged me from the very beginning and never doubted that it was good enough. Also thanks to her for being the 4-H and Pony Club person and sharing the history of the equestrian park.

Members of my book group were also obliging and allowed me to choose my own unpublished work when it was my turn to pick a book. Thanks to Kathy Ostrom, Bekah Townsend, Lin Holley, Anne Bell, Michael Butler, Patty McKinnon, Susan Bates, Sheila Eckman, and Amy Huggins for being so very positive and helpful in their remarks.

Other readers were Mary Litchfield Tuel, Ivette Silberman, Janet Meskin, and Cynthia Golfus. I notice suddenly that there are only women listed here. I did give the manuscript to a few men, but they, sadly, never got back to me about it.

My dear long-time friend Nancy Morgan turns out to be a wonderful editor and proofreader, and she recommended Natalie Kosovac as a designer. Thanks to those two it actually looks like a real book!

Henna Volker, my talented daughter-in-law, drew the chapter heading illustrations.

The cover photo deserves special mention—it is the Tie-Dye Master and Natural Philosopher himself holding up the jacket he made for me. Thanks, Rod Smith.

About the Author

PHOTO ©JIM MEIKLEJOHN

Rebecca Graves moved from Memphis, Tennessee to Vashon Island, Washington in 1975. A teacher with a master's degree in early childhood education, she has been engaged in that profession in various ways—from teaching preschool and kindergarten, to doing neurodevelopmental therapy, to substitute teaching. She is heavily involved in community and the arts, singing with the Threshold Choir and two other choruses, participating in fiber arts groups with knitting and felting, producing a fundraiser for the high school drama department that brought in $12,000, and creating a popular Facebook page called Visual Delights on Vashon, where locals showcase their photographs of the beauty that surrounds us.

She has been married to Phil Volker for forty years and they have raised two children, Tesia and Wiley.

CPSIA information can be obtained
at www.ICGtesting.com
Printed in the USA
FSHW021255151119
64141FS

9 780578 539102